I0632735

A Father's Love

by

Sherry Derr Wille

Published by
Melange Books, LLC
White Bear Lake, MN 55110
www.melange-books.com

A Father's Love ~ Copyright © 2014 by Sherry Derr Wille

ISBN: 978-1-61235-895-6

Names, characters, and incidents depicted in this book are products of the author's imagination or are used fictitiously. Any resemblance to actual events, locales, organizations, or persons, living or dead, is entirely coincidental and beyond the intent of the author or the publisher. No part of this book may be reproduced or transmitted in any form or by any means, electronic or mechanical, including photocopying, recording, or by any information storage and retrieval system, without permission in writing from the publisher.
Published in the United States of America.

Cover Art by Caroline Andrus

A Father's Love
Sherry Derr Wille

When Jenny found herself pregnant at the age of fifteen she thought her life was over, but with supportive parents, she was able to get her education. With her future secure at the hospital on the reservation where she grew up, love was the last thing she wanted in her life.

Brand knew he was going to be practicing in a rural hospital. What he didn't realize that Jenny, the beautiful Native American girl who entered his life would become so special to him he would become a doctor at the Lac du Flambeau reservation in Northern Wisconsin to be close to her.

I dedicate this book to everyone who has ever gone against convention and married for love rather than to satisfy the requirements of their family and friends.

Prologue

Lac du Flambeau Reservation Wisconsin - 1998

Jennifer Red Hawk left the free clinic, her thoughts in turmoil. A glance in the plate glass window of the store next to the clinic told her she looked like any other sixteen-year-old girl on the Lac du Flambeau reservation in northern Wisconsin. Her blue-black hair hung in long braids down her back and her bronze skin and dark brown eyes attested to her Native American heritage. She looked no different than she had before the doctor diagnosed the mysterious illness that made her feel run down all summer.

How could she be pregnant? At sixteen, she still had her junior and senior years of high school ahead of her, to say nothing of college.

Instead of going home, she made her way to Charlie Little Horse's home. They went together throughout the past school year. On the night of Charlie's graduation party, they slipped away, and he took her out to the lake. Once there, he talked her into having sex in the back seat of his father's car. He'd assured her she couldn't get pregnant the first time they had sex and besides all the girls did it. Like a fool, she believed him.

She knew other girls who got pregnant and dropped out of school, but they weren't her. They were the girls her mother called 'fast and loose', they certainly weren't Jennifer who never disobeyed her parents, went to church on Sunday, and planned to go to college to become a nurse when she finished high school.

She found Charlie playing football in the front yard with his friends. When he saw her, he left the others to carry on and walked her to the back

1

of the house. Once alone, he pulled her into his arms and kissed her hungrily. She knew what would come next. He would put his hand inside her blouse and play with her breasts until she could hardly stand it. Then he would demand sex. Since the first time when the pain had been almost unbearable, she found herself unable to fend him off, for all the good it did her.

"Did you come to give me my going away present, baby?" he said as he groped at her breast. "The folks are having a special dinner for me, but I'll be free after eight. If you come back then we can make love under the stars."

Jenny pulled away. "I didn't come for that. I came to tell you I'm pregnant."

She watched his face, expecting to see … to see what? Shock, horror, embarrassment, or compassion?

"Who's the lucky guy?"

The question came as a shock and yet it wasn't unexpected. It was what most guys would have said until they got used to the idea.

"You are, and you know it."

"Hell, baby, one word from me and ten guys will swear they've been with you."

"But you can't. It would be a lie."

"Don't you realize it would be your word against mine? Who do you think they'll believe? I'm Ben Little Horse's son and you're nothing. Your father is only one of my dad's workers. Without that job, where do you think your family would be?"

Jenny stood staring at him in a state of shock. "But … but what about our baby?"

"Your baby, honey. It's best you get your pronouns right. This is your problem. I won't even be around to consider such a thing. I'm leaving in the morning for the UW at Milwaukee. I've got a bright future ahead of me. I'm not going to let a little bitch like you ruin it for me. Have a nice life, but don't go trying to pin your brat on me. If you do, you'll be sorry."

Charlie turned his back on her and walked away. Tears filled Jenny's eyes. Without Charlie by her side, she would have to face her parents alone. She stayed in the backyard for several minutes until she saw Charlie's mother coming from the house.

A Father's Love

"Jenny, why don't you come in the house and help me with supper. We have plenty, and you're more than welcome to stay."

"Thank you, Mrs. Little Horse, but I have to get home. I promised Mama I'd help her get supper for us. She's counting on me. I just stopped to tell Charlie good-bye before he leaves for school tomorrow."

"I understand. I just don't know why he thinks he has to get there two weeks early. It will be quiet around here, but I'll get used to it. Don't you be a stranger. I have work to do, so I'll be seeing you."

Jenny relaxed her forced smile and cut across the backyards of houses that belonged to her friends, praying she wouldn't run into anyone she knew until she returned home.

The screen door slammed behind her as she made her way to the kitchen. Her mother was making hamburger patties for the picnic supper they had planned all week and her father was chopping the onions.

"Can I talk to you and Daddy?" Jenny said, drawing her parents' attention to her.

"What's wrong Jen?" her father said as her mother hurried to her side.

"Oh Mama, Daddy, I'm pregnant." She knew she shouldn't have just blurted it out like that, but the words escaped before she could stop them.

Anger clouded her father's usually laughing brown eyes. "Who is the father, that little bastard, Charlie Little Horse?"

Jenny nodded, tears streaming down her cheeks. "It was the night of his graduation party, after everyone else went home, we went down to the lake. He said I couldn't get pregnant the first time and I believed him. He said it made his graduation special."

"I'm going over there. Hold off on that picnic until I get back, Betsy."

Jenny put her hand on her father's arm. "Don't waste your time, Daddy. I went there first. Charlie is leaving for Milwaukee tomorrow for school. He said if I went to his father, he'd deny the baby is his. He also said there were a lot of his friends who would say they'd been with me, even though that's a lie. He told me if I made a fuss, he'd make certain you'd lose your job."

Her father's shoulders slumped in defeat.

"Jenny's right, Tom. We can't do anything until this baby is born. Once it is, we can prove Charlie is the father. Jenny isn't the first of our people to be in this situation. I should know. I was just her age when I had

Matthew. It was hard for me because my family wasn't supportive. I had to quit school, and if you hadn't agreed to marry me and raise a child that wasn't yours, I don't know what I would have done. I won't let my daughter give up on her dream of going to school and making something of herself. No matter what it takes, we'll make certain she gets the education she deserves."

Jenny watched as her father took her mother in his arms to give her comfort. In her wildest dreams, Jenny never thought her older brother didn't have the same father as she, her younger brother, and sister did. She wondered if he knew. Not that it mattered. Tom Red Hawk was a good father to all of his children. It didn't matter to him about Matthew not being his natural son. Maybe someday her child would have such a father in his life.

"Your mother's right. You're my little girl and I love you dearly. I still want to beat some sense into Charlie, but your welfare comes first. Times are different now than when your mother found out she was pregnant with your brother. You won't have to quit school. I want you to go on to college, and if it means your mother and I will be raising your child, so be it. Your mother missed so much of her youth that I refuse to put you through the same thing."

* * * *

By the time school started in September, Jenny could tell that her normally flat stomach was beginning to swell with pregnancy. Other girls in her class were pregnant and still others were no longer in school because their parents weren't supportive.

As her condition became evident, more and more of her friends asked who the father was. After Charlie's threat, she was reluctant to name him. It was hard to keep his identity a secret, but she knew it was necessary. She couldn't risk the chance of her father losing his job and not be able to keep his word about helping her to continue her schooling despite the child that now kicked her ribs constantly.

The last day of school before Christmas vacation brought a heavy snow to the northern Wisconsin reservation. Trudging home, Jenny watched as boys teased girls with snowballs and younger kids ran ahead of her skidding across patches of hidden ice beneath the newly fallen snow.

4

A Father's Love

When she slipped, Jenny was surprised to feel a pair of strong arms steadying her before she could fall. She was unprepared to see Charlie's farther holding her in his arms.

"I've been waiting for you," Ben Little Horse said. "We've missed seeing you at the house."

Jenny hung her head, ashamed of her condition and the reason she hadn't visited Charlie's parents since he left for school in August. "I didn't know if I'd be welcome in your home."

He looked down at the bump of her pregnancy protruding from beneath her coat.

"Does the child you're carrying, belong to Charlie?"

Jenny nodded. "He denied it. My parents are helping me. They're going to raise my child so I can finish high school and go on to college like my brother, Matt."

"I heard he was doing well at Platteville. Will he be coming home for Christmas break?"

"Matt should be home later tonight. How about Charlie? When is he due to get home?"

"He's spending Christmas with some friends he made at school. If the truth were known, he's ashamed of his heritage. He sent home a photo and he's cut his hair and bleached it blond. Take this and get something for the baby."

He pressed something into her hand and walked away. When she looked down, she saw three one hundred dollar bills held together with a paper clip resting in the palm of her mitten.

"What did old man Little Horse want with you?" her younger sister, Leslie said.

Jenny shoved the bills inside her mitten before turning to face her sister. "I slipped on the ice, and he kept me from falling."

"Well, that's a shock. If you'd fallen, you might have lost the baby. If that happened, he wouldn't ever have to admit it's his grandchild. Like father, like son, that's what Daddy says."

Jenny remained silent. She knew all about what her father said concerning the things going on in the village, especially the ones Ben Little Horse orchestrated. There was a powerful hatred between the two of them. Whatever originally caused it, she knew her pregnancy made it worse.

* * * *

Christmas proved to be a joyous time, but it also signaled the beginning of Jenny's third trimester of pregnancy. Matt played big brother until it the time came for him to go back to school and complete his final year of college. In the spring, he would be getting his engineering degree. Now that Jenny knew the truth about her parents and Matt, she understood the reason for the six-year difference in their ages. She wondered if he knew as well.

"A penny for your thoughts, Sis," Matt said one night before he was scheduled to return to school.

Jenny put her hand protectively over her belly and felt the baby kick. "I was just wondering what kind of life I'll be able to give to my baby."

"With Mom and Dad on your side, the two of you will be just fine. I remember what it was like for Mom before Dad married her."

"You knew?"

"Of course I did. I was four, and I remember living in a shack on the other side of the tracks. When Mom had to go to work every day to support us, I stayed with a babysitter who was quick to point out I was a bastard. Even at four, I knew what the name meant because she explained it to me in no uncertain terms. When Dad got back from the army, he started dating Mom. I remember telling him I was a bastard and he couldn't have my mother without having me. He told me he'd already started legal procedures to make me his forever. They make a great team, and your baby will never suffer. If need be, Dad will adopt him, but I don't think that's what you want."

"No, it's not, but I'm looking at four years of college before I can become a registered nurse, to say nothing of finishing high school. By the time I'm able to come back here and make a home for the two of us, he'll be ready for school."

* * * *

On Valentine's Day, Jenny's labor began. Her mother, along with the midwife, helped her get ready for the birth of her child. Even with the people she trusted by her side, Jenny was frightened. She wasn't due for

6

another two weeks and thoughts of a premature birth were foremost in her mind.

Hours later the lusty cry of a newborn baby filled Jenny's bedroom. The months of pregnancy and the hours of labor had produced a perfectly formed, six-pound, thirteen-ounce baby boy.

As Jenny cuddled her son she searched his face for traces of the boy who planted the seed needed to form the baby. She silently thanked God her son, Alex, looked more like her own father rather than his. Even though Charlie's father knew Alex was his grandson, Jenny understood he planned to shield his wife from the knowledge her son didn't want to accept the responsibilities of fatherhood.

Life would never be easy for her, but she knew her parents would not allow either her or her son to suffer because of Charlie's indifference and unwillingness to accept his responsibilities.

Chapter One

The University of Wisconsin, Madison, 2004

Brand Masterson pulled up in front of Fredrick Hall. He'd been lucky to get a dorm room here. With the close proximity to the hospital, it was perfect for him. He knew most residents preferred to get apartments off campus, but Brand thought the extra expense was unnecessary. In the last year of his residency, he knew he wouldn't be spending much time in an apartment, and he didn't mind having a roommate.

Earlier, he'd helped his sister Frannie move into this same building. She was finishing her nurses training and, like him, wanted to be close to the hospital. Her decision had been helped along because his roommate, Greg Thomas, had been dating her for the past year and a half. After they both graduated in the spring they were planning to get married and settle wherever he started his practice.

Brand came down from the fourth floor where his room gave him a spectacular view of the lake and hurried out the door for yet another load of his belongings. With his mind elsewhere, he didn't notice the young woman coming into the building until he ran into her knocking the box she was carrying to the ground.

"I'm so sorry," Brand said as he bent to help her retrieve the spilled contents of the box. "I wasn't watching where I was going."

"That's all right, neither was I," she replied, her voice sounding like the sweet song of a bird.

He took a moment to look at her closely. Her hair was long and hung down her back like a blue/black curtain and her skin had a delicate bronze hue telling him she either spent the summer in the sun or she had a Native

American heritage. When Frannie got the notice of her roommate for the year, she learned the girl's name would be Jennifer Red Hawk. She had good legs too in those cut offs.

"I'm Brand Masterson. The way it looks we're both going to be rooming here this term."

She smiled as she accepted his outstretched hand. "Jennifer Red Hawk, but my friends call me Jenny. The name Masterson sounds familiar. You wouldn't be related to Francine Masterson, would you?"

"Only slightly, she's my younger sister. You must be her roommate. Frannie was really excited about rooming with you. She's been over the top about you being Native American. She's really into going to pow-wows and learning everything she can about the culture. Would I be too forward to ask you which tribe you're from?"

"You wouldn't. I'm Chippewa from the Lac du Flambeau reservation."

She reached for the cardboard box he held in his hands, but he wouldn't yield his hold on it.

"Allow me, pretty lady. I would enjoy playing tour guide and show you to your room."

She nodded acceptance of his offer and pulled open the door so they could both enter the lobby. Once they were in the elevator, he pushed the button for the third floor.

After the doors opened, he guided her down the hall to the corner room she would be sharing with Frannie.

"I ran into your roommate, Sis," he called as he entered the room. "I hope you're decent."

"Of course I am," Frannie replied as she came out of the bathroom. "You have to be Jennifer. I'm so pleased to finally meet you."

"Jenny," the woman who had captured his imagination corrected.

"Toss me your keys, Jenny, and I'll bring up the rest of your stuff," Brand offered.

"Oh, I couldn't ask you to do that."

"You didn't ask. If I'm not mistaken, you had a long drive to get here. You have to be tired. It's the least I can do for a fellow student. How much stuff do you have in your car?"

"I have most everything in this box. There's only a laptop and a really big suitcase."

"Good then I'll save you a couple of trips."

He smiled as Jenny reached into the pocket of her cut offs and pulled out a set of keys. The fact she took him up on his offer was a good sign he might have a chance at a date with her sometime in the near future.

* * * *

Jenny watched Brand leave the room and pull the door shut behind him. "Is your brother for real?"

"You mean Brand? Of course he is. He's a real Sir Walter Raleigh. Watch out for him, he could easily become a ladies' man. Still, I hope he'll have more time for socializing this year than he did last year. That means his roommate, Greg, will have time to spend with me."

"Why wouldn't they have off time?"

"They're in the last year of their residencies. In the spring, they'll be graduating and finding places to practice. Wherever Greg goes, that where I'll be as well. We're getting married next spring." Frannie held up her left hand to show off the diamond ring on her third finger for emphasis. "I'll wait to see where he ends up before I put out feelers for a job. How about you? Do you have any idea where you'll be working?"

"I got some great scholarships not only from the reservation where my parents live, but also from the hospital there. I'll have a position waiting for me at the hospital once I get my RN."

"Don't you want to go somewhere exotic, farther away from home?"

"Madison is exotic enough for me. Besides, my family and my people need me there. I have a son, and I'd never take him away from our people."

"You have a son?" Frannie looked surprised. "How old is he?"

Jenny reached into the box and pulled out the picture her brother had taken of the two of them when they were out fishing this summer. "He's five. He's starting kindergarten next week. I really hate to miss his first day of school, but my folks promised to take lots of pictures of him. I can hardly wait to have them show up in my inbox."

Frannie took the picture and studied Alex's strong features. "He looks like you."

Jenny was again glad that Alex closely resembled her father and not Charlie. She hadn't heard from Charlie since the day he left her standing in the backyard of his home wondering how she would raise her child alone. She heard the gossip spreading through the reservation about him. He'd gone to Milwaukee to school and gotten caught up with the wrong people.

From what she'd heard, his father had paid plenty to two other women who were more vocal about the father of their children. The story she heard said Ben paid them off when they threatened to sue him. It was all very hush-hush, but the rumors still ran rampant.

Fortunately, as far as Alex was concerned, he liked that her brother Matt shared not having a father. Even though he rarely mentioned it, she knew he envied the few friends he had with both a mother and father to raise them.

"He's a good looking boy. You must have been very young when he was born. How did you ever manage taking care of a kid and getting your education at the same time?'

"My folks insisted I should finish my education and not give up on my dream of becoming a nurse. They've raised Alex. He's not all that much younger than my youngest brother, so it's like they have another kid. He knows they are grandma and grandpa and that I'm his mother. He sends me e-mails every day to tell me what he's doing."

"He can write e-mails?" Frannie sounded surprised.

Jenny laughed at the question. "No, but my mother can. He tells her what he wants to say, and she types it in word for word. They're fun to read. I like to imagine it's him writing them and not my mother."

"Open the door before I drop from exhaustion," Brand called from outside the closed door.

Jenny hurried to open it. She'd become so lost in talking with Frannie, she'd forgotten Brand went downstairs to bring up her things.

"How did you think you were going to get this thing up here?" Brand said. "This suitcase weighs a ton. What do you have in there, bricks?"

"Hardly. I picked up some used text books for this year's classes from E-bay. It sure beats paying full price for them. Besides, with the wheels on my bag it wouldn't have been much of a job. The worst part would have been getting it out of the car."

"All I can say is thank goodness I'm almost all moved in and so is Frannie. I don't think I could make many more treks for the rest of our belongings. I'll let you girls get better acquainted while I go up and get settled. Greg should be here soon, and I know he'll need help too. He always brings more things than he needs."

"You're exaggerating again, Big Brother. Greg doesn't over pack."

"Maybe not, but it makes for a good story. What time did he tell you he'd be here?"

"The last e-mail I got before I left home said he was planning to get here around three. He said he wanted to go out to dinner tonight at TJ Whitney's. You know how much he loves those raspberry ribs."

"I don't blame him. Do you like raspberry ribs, Jenny?" Brand said.

"I don't know. I've never had them. I don't socialize much. I usually have too much studying to do."

Brand reached over and took Jenny's hand. Just his touch made her heart flutter. This wasn't what she wanted. She was first and foremost a mother with a five-year-old son to consider. She didn't need a man in her life complicating things. Her mother had been lucky to find a man as good as her dad to give her son a father, but Jenny doubted a white man would want to be saddled with a Native American child whose father wanted nothing to do with him.

"Since classes don't begin until tomorrow, there's no studying for you to do tonight. I'd be pleased if you'd be my guest for the evening. Someone has to chaperone my dear sister and Greg. There's nothing to stop me from enjoying the evening as much as they do."

"I … I couldn't. I don't know you and you don't know me. I'm not the kind of girl you should be dating. I'm sure—"

Brand's smile was unnerving. "I'm just as sure you're the girl I want to be with tonight. I don't care if you're red, yellow, blue, or purple. You're a lovely woman, and I'm looking forward to spending an enjoyable evening with you. Who knows how many nights I'll be available after I start my shifts at the hospital.

"If Greg is getting in at three, we'll pick you girls up at six. Be ready for a night of celebrating. This is the last year for Greg and me as well as the last year for both of you. Consider this your last fling before all the hard work starts. I've been told the work load for your senior year is murder, and combined with the time you're on the floor, you'll be too exhausted to party."

Jenny watched as Brand left the dorm room. "Is he serious?"

"He's very serious. I can see that he's taken with you."

"How can he be? We've only just met. He doesn't know anything about me."

"Go with the flow, Jenny. If Brand wants to show you a good time, take advantage of it. After tonight we'll have tons of homework and not a lot of free time. Besides, it's just a date. He hasn't asked you to sleep with him."

Jenny nodded. "I guess you're right. I haven't done any dating since my son was born. I got burned once, and I'm not looking forward to having such a thing happen again."

"I can understand how you feel. It sounds like your son's father was a real jerk with a capital J. My first boyfriend was like that. When I wouldn't go to bed with him, he dumped me like a hot potato and told everyone I was a cold fish. He was out to ruin me, and for a while he did. I didn't do any other dating until I got to college. Of course, when I met Greg, I knew my dating days were over. He's my one true love. Thank goodness my parents like him almost as much as I do."

Jenny agreed and began to unpack. She found a pair of jeans and a top she considered flattering to her small figure and decided they would be perfect for going to TJ Whitney's. While she'd been at the UW, she'd heard her classmates talking about the restaurant and mini brewery where they were going tonight. She'd tried not to feel jealous of her carefree friends. For them college was a social experience with the benefit of what they were learning as just a perk. For her, getting her degree and becoming an RN was the most important thing in her life. With it, she would have the means to care for and support her son without any help from the man who fathered him. Since Charlie didn't want anything to do with either her or Alex, so be it. She would be both his mother and father, but not without the education she was working so hard to complete

* * * *

Greg arrived at ten after three and after getting settled, took his time in the shower, while Brand shaved for the second time in one day. He couldn't believe his luck at having literally run into Jenny this afternoon. Her Native American heritage made her an exotic beauty and a girl he wanted to get to know better.

"So what's Frannie's roommate like?" Greg said, as soon as his belongings were strewn over half the room.

"The word angel isn't strong enough to describe her. She's beautiful and at the same time so naive she doesn't even know what her effect on a guy really is. When I asked her out, she acted like I'd lost my mind for wanting to go out with her."

"Maybe she's just shy."

"I hope that's all it is. I'd hate to think she has some unspeakable disease. Oh, and did I tell you that she's Native American?"

"Only about six times. Of course, Jenny is all Frannie has been talking about ever since she got her rooming assignment. I'm really looking forward to meeting this chick. She really has to be something to get the two of you so worked up."

"She certainly is. I think this is going to be a very exciting year. I can hardly believe my good luck to have her living in the same dorm with us. I think our off time will be extremely interesting this year."

"For your sake I hope so. As I recall, last year you were working your butt off and refused even to let me set you up with someone. I was beginning to worry about you my friend."

Chapter Two

"Are you ready?" Frannie called from outside the closed bathroom door. "The guys will be here any minute."

"I'm not going," Jenny called back.

The mirror over the sink reflected the tears running down her cheeks. She wasn't like Frannie. She could never be a carefree young woman. She had a child to think about. Alex needed a mother who was prepared to support him. She needed to concentrate on her studies, not party. She'd made it through three years of college without giving into the temptation that gave her Alex five years earlier.

"You can't back out on us. Brand is looking forward to being with you tonight," Frannie said as she opened the door to invade Jenny's private moment of self-pity.

"What's there to look forward to? He hardly knows me, and when he does get to know me, he'll find out about Alex. Once he does, he won't want anything to do with me. Why should I even try? I'm nothing but a little Indian whore, and everyone knows it."

"Who told you such a thing?"

"Alex's father. Only he used different words. When I told him I was pregnant, he said he'd have his buddies all say they'd been with me. I know what they say on the reservation about girls who get pregnant without being married. They all said it about me. I was one of the lucky ones. My parents supported me, and I've been able to get my education in spite of being an unwed mother."

"I know what you're talking about. Our older sister went through the same thing. She was fifteen when she got pregnant. I remember all the things people said about her, but Mom and Dad told her things like that happen and she should hold her head high. It was hard, but she gave her baby up for adoption. It was one of those open adoptions, so she gets to see him regularly. He knows she's his birth mom but she loved him enough to give him two parents to take care of him. "My mom wouldn't have been able to take care of a little one. You're so lucky with the kind of parents you have. I know it hurts my sister when she sees Michael with his folks.

"As for Brand, don't be afraid. He's known lots of girls who have been in the same situation as you are. Most of them are struggling. You're different. You've given yourself permission to make something of your life. I think you deserve a lot of credit. So tonight, should be a celebration of your take charge look at life."

"I still don't know. What will I say? How will I ever explain to him about Alex?"

"The same way you explained to me. Now hurry up. I saw the outfit you laid out on the bed, and I think it looks perfect for tonight."

Jenny turned back to the mirror and studied her face. The tears were dried but her eyes were red. Instead of continuing to feel sorry for herself and hide from the truth, she washed her face and reapplied her makeup. For one night she was going to have a good time.

* * * *

"This is going to be a great night," Greg said as he came out of the bathroom. He'd changed into a pair of white jeans with a brightly colored shirt. He looked like something out of a movie about Hawaii.

"I take it that's something you picked up on vacation this summer," Brand teased.

"As a matter of fact it is. The folks decided it would be the last family vacation, since next year at this time I'm going to be married and starting a practice in God only knows where."

"Just remember, that shirt isn't some chick magnet. It's my sister you're going out with and planning to marry."

"Like how could I forget? I was so lonely for her while we were gone I could hardly wait to get back to school. Now that has to be love. So don't keep me waiting any longer. You have to know I just flew in this morning, and I haven't even had a chance to see my one and only girl."

Brand smiled at Greg and grabbed the moleskin jacket he's gotten for Christmas. It was lightweight enough to be worn year round, making it the perfect companion to his jeans and sport shirt for an evening out at TJ Whitney's. Even though he could almost taste the raspberry ribs for which the restaurant was so famous, he knew tonight would be special. Tonight he would be with Jenny and nothing else mattered.

By the time he got to the room Jenny shared with his sister, Greg was already playing kissy face with Frannie. Behind her, he could see Jenny standing shyly in the room as though embarrassed by the show of affection between his sister and his roommate.

"You'll learn to ignore the two of them," Brand said, as he pushed past Greg and Frannie to enter. "They're in love and it does get a bit sickening at times. Of course, you'll eventually get used to it. I don't know why the two of them didn't get a room together and save us all a lot of embarrassment."

Jenny looked at him as though he'd lost his mind, but she'd get used to his ways. He wanted her in his life, at least for this school year. In the past, he'd dated a lot of girls and for him one date was enough. After seeing Jenny a few hours earlier, he'd made up his mind that she was someone he wanted to know better.

"There's nothing to ignore. They're in love and are going to be married. They have every right to show their affection."

"Have you ever been in love, Jenny?"

They had reached the car, and she waited for him to open the car door before she answered his question. From the look on her face, he knew that the answer was yes and her heart had been broken. Even with her coppery complexion, he could see the hint of a blush on her cheeks.

"I thought I was, but to him I was only a conquest. He went off to college and forgot I ever existed. The problem is I couldn't forget. I have to be honest with you. I have a five-year-old son. He'll be starting kindergarten in a few days."

Brand sat for a moment in silence as he digested that information. "Does his father ever see him?" he finally managed to ask.

"He doesn't even acknowledge Alex. My son's name is Alex. Thankfully, my parents dote on him. My folks have given him a good home. Charlie's parents are very wealthy, and his father sends money to help. Charlie's mother doesn't even know she has a grandson. Mom and Dad put the money from Charlie's dad in an account in Alex's name, but they did allow Ben to get Alex his school supplies and clothes."

"So, where is this jerk?"

"His father doesn't say much about him other than he's had to pay for at least two abortions for girls Charlie got in trouble. He was going to school in Milwaukee, but I don't think he ever graduated. The last I knew, he was selling cars in Chicago. What a waste. My own brother was going to college at the same time and he brought back his knowledge to the reservation, at least until he got an offer from a firm in Appleton he couldn't turn down. I guess Charlie is ashamed of being Chippewa."

"Why in the world would he be ashamed of something so special?" Greg asked from the back seat. "I think it would be great to have Indian blood."

"It should be, but Native Americans get a really bad rap. Everyone looks at us like we're going on the warpath at any minute. We don't go around scalping people or raiding village, and we aren't all lazy drunks. I'm proud of my heritage, and I'm working to make my son proud of it as well. I speak our native language and so does he, but we also speak English because it is the language of this country. We're good Americans but we're also good Chippewa. I'll understand if none of you want anything more to do with me. I'm used to it. This is my last year in Madison. Once I graduate, I'll go back where I belong. I can do more for my people with an education than I can without it."

Brand reached across the console to grasp her hand. He knew it took a lot of courage for her to admit she'd been a mother at such a young age. She couldn't have been any more than sixteen when she gave birth. It had to have been hard to take on the responsibility of a child, even with the support of her parents.

"You have plenty to be proud of," Brand assured her. "I give you a lot of credit for keeping your baby. From what I hear, too many Native American children have been adopted by white parents and have lost their heritage. That's the problem with our society; too many of us have no idea of what our background is or where we came from. I wish we did, but other things are more important in our lives."

"I agree," Greg said. "I know my father's family came from England and my mother has German and Irish blood, but that's about all I know. My cousin is digging into the history of the family, but until you mentioned it, I never gave where I came from much thought. At least you know where your roots are planted and your background. The rest of us are little more than mongrels. We have more heritage than we can shake a stick at, but we don't know exactly what it is."

Brand sensed Jenny relax. It was possible the four of them would be comfortable with each other now that everything about Jenny was out in the open.

* * * *

Jenny enjoyed the restaurant her new friends chose. The ribs were some of the best she'd ever tasted, and the company was exceptional. Greg and Frannie were totally obsessed with each other, and Brand spent the evening asking her about her dreams as well as Alex.

In exchange, he told her he was looking forward to graduation and practicing medicine.

"Where are you looking to go for a job?" Jenny said.

"I don't know just yet. I'll have to see what's out there once I graduate. I know I don't want to work for one of the big clinics or hospitals. I've always wanted to be a good old country doctor. You know, someone who makes house calls and actually knows his patients."

"That surprises me. I could see you in one of the big hospitals, like St. Mary's or Meriter in Madison."

"No, they're way too big to suit me. Frannie and I are from a small town, and I've seen what those big hospitals are like in our area. People are no more than numbers, and the insurance companies sometimes compromise the care they get. You've seen how they shuffle people in and out of the hospital before they should. I worked on the transplant floor last year and was shocked to see those patients going home in a week. Back several years ago, people stayed at least three weeks and got the education they needed to take care of themselves when they returned home. I don't want that for my patients. Even if their insurance sends them home too early, I want to be able to stay in touch with them and find out how they're doing on a day to day basis."

"It sounds like you'd like Dr. Hawk. He's one of the head honchos at the hospital on the reservation."

"I take it he's Native American, like you."

"Not quite. He is Native American and comes from the Dakotas. He and his wife met while he was serving in a MASH unit in Vietnam. I worked for him when I was in high school and when I came home for vacations. When I get home, I'll have a position at the reservation hospital."

"It's great you have goals that fulfill needs. My only goal is I want get through this year and put MD behind my name. I feel like I've had a great opportunity being able to study at this hospital. It will look good on my resume."

Jenny suspected even though Brand said he didn't want to work for one of the big hospitals, he didn't mean it. She'd met a lot of doctors during her schooling and most of them wouldn't do well in a small setting like the one she would return to once she completed her degree. She could imagine Brand working in a prestigious clinic or at a large hospital in a major city. No matter what he said, he wasn't someone who would be content living just barely above the poverty line working in a small town.

Chapter Three

```
Dear Mommy
     Today I went to school. My friend, Jason
Straight  Arrow,  was  there,  too.  We  had  a
good  time.  Our  teacher  is  Mrs.  Eagle.  She
is very nice.
     Alex
```

Jenny smiled at the e-mail. Janet Eagle had been the kindergarten teacher on the reservation for the past twenty-five years. She remembered her teacher as a tiny woman who enjoyed painting with watercolors and teaching the children who came through her classroom. Jenny stayed in contact with her all through her high school years as well as after she started college. If anyone could instill a love of learning in her son it was Janet Eagle.

```
Dear Alex
     I'm  so  proud  of  you.  You  couldn't  have  a
better  teacher  than  Mrs.  Eagle.  I  know  you
will  do  your  best  in  her  class.  My  classes
are  going  well  and  by  the  end  of  the  year
we  will  be  together  all  the  time.  I  can
hardly  wait  until  we  can  find  our  own
house,  one  with  a  nice  yard,  where  you  can
play with your friends.
```

```
Love Mommy
```

She added the last part for her parents. She knew they were interested in her life while in school at Madison. Since she knew they wouldn't approve of her seeing someone like Brand, she purposely neglected to say anything to them about him. As long as she kept up her grades, she decided not to let on her social life changed from its status for the past three years.

Her computer dinged, signaling that another message had come in. This one was from her brother.

```
Hi Jen
    How's it going this year? I hope you're
finding time for things other than your
studies. I know Mom and Dad haven't said
anything to you about it, but they're
worried. They don't think you have a social
life and believe me it's something
important. I have business in Madison this
weekend. Do you think you could paint the
town with your big brother?
    Matt
```

Jenny thought about her date with Brand tonight. He had the weekend off and so did she. He would want to make plans for the two of them. How could she tell him to get lost because her brother was coming to town and wouldn't understand why she was going out with a white guy?

```
Matt
    I'm looking forward to seeing you this
weekend. Are you bringing anyone special
with you? Mom says there's a young lady in
your life. I'd like to meet her.
    Jen
```

Matt's reply came back within moments.

I'd love to oblige you, but Karen isn't quite ready to meet my family. She's white, and worried what you'll think of her.

Jenny breathed a sigh of relief.

Let's plan a double date. I'm seeing a white guy too. I didn't know how to break this to you. Guess this is the best way for both of us. Why don't you meet me at the Memorial Union on Saturday morning? Brand and I both have the weekend off. We can make a day of it. Let me know if eleven is too early for you.

"Are you ready to go?" Brand called from outside the door. "The movie starts in an hour and a half so we have just enough time to grab something to eat."

Jenny hurried to open the door. As much as she wanted to wait for a reply from Matt, she knew Brand was right. By the time they stopped for pizza and got to the movie, the feature would be ready to begin. This was one movie she wanted to see.

"I just have to get a jacket," she said when Brand entered the room.

Before she could turn back to the bed where she had left her jacket, Brand pulled her into his arms and kissed her. "Are you sure we have to go out? Greg and Frannie aren't anywhere around. We could make our own fun right here."

"Not on your life. I made that mistake once and I won't make it again. I promised myself I wouldn't get sucked into anything like being sexually serious until I was properly married."

Brand pulled her into his arms and kissed her again. "I'm glad my sister and roommate haven't corrupted you. I'm as anxious as you are to get to the movies. As for sex before marriage, I don't approve of it either."

Jenny picked up her jacket and allowed Brand to hold the door for her. "Do you still have this weekend off?" she said once they were in his car and heading toward Rocky Rococo's Pizza.

"That's right, it's the only one this month. Since you have it off too, is there something special you want to do?"

It was now or never. She had to tell him about Matt coming to Madison. "I just had an e-mail from my brother. He's coming to Madison on business this weekend and wants to get together."

"What kind of business would he have here on the weekend?"

"Probably none, but it's a good excuse for the two of us to get together. He's an architect in Appleton. If there were business here in town, it wouldn't be until next week. Something tells me this is a trip to assure him I'm not being a wallflower while I'm here. He said my parents are worried about my lack of a social life. I didn't have any choice but to tell him about you."

Brand grew unnaturally silent.

"He wants to meet you," she continued hoping to establish a conversation about Brand meeting Matt. "I'm hopeful he'll going to bring his girlfriend along this weekend."

"Are you sure you want me to meet him? I don't know if I'm exactly the kind of guy your family would approve of for you."

"If it makes you feel any better, Matt is dating a white girl. I just sent him an e-mail suggesting he bring her along and we make it a double date. Now are you more comfortable?"

He reached over and squeezed her hand. "It sounds like he's got an open mind. At least it won't be like meeting your parents. I have a feeling they might not be as understanding as someone who's dating a white woman."

Jenny smiled at his comment. It was true, her parents wouldn't be too happy about her dating someone who wasn't Native American, but she'd dated Charlie and what had it gotten her? She wouldn't trade Alex for anything in the world, but it would have been better if his father had married her and loved and supported her and his child.

A Father's Love

* * * *

Brand worried about the weekend date with Jenny's brother and his girlfriend, but he didn't say anything. It seemed important to Jenny, so he didn't want to spoil the weekend for her. Her background made no difference to him or his family, but he suspected her family felt differently. As much as he cared for Jenny, he assumed her family wouldn't immediately accept him.

Once they returned home from the movie, Brand kissed her goodnight and hurried up to his room. He needed advice and knew he couldn't get it from Jenny or anyone else at the dorm. He would send an e-mail to his friend Cindy. They dated in high school, but went their separate ways when they left for college.

While she was in college in San Francisco, she had met and fallen in love with David Chi, who was second generation Chinese/American. Brand knew her family had been against an interracial marriage, and David's family was less than thrilled with his white girlfriend.

Brand had attended the wedding and watched as the families glared at each other across the aisle of the church. It proved to be an interesting wedding to say the least. Cindy's Lutheran minister shared the pulpit with a Buddhist monk, even though David parents had converted to Christianity years earlier. The monk came as the request of David's grandparents.

David won over Cindy's parents and his parents came to love her, but David's grandparents were a whole other story. They'd decided years earlier not to learn how to speak English and communicated with the family and everyone else through an interpreter.

It took the birth of their first great-grandchild to for them to come to love and accept Cindy into their family.

As soon as his computer came to life, he opened his Internet connection and pulled up the compose box for his e-mail.

```
Hi Cindy
     Didn't think I'd ever be writing to you
about something like this, but I need your
advice. I've met a girl and she's different
from anyone I've ever known. She's Native
American and although I know my parents
```

won't have a problem with her, I'm not so
certain about her family accepting me. I'm
meeting her brother this weekend. Can you
give me any suggestions about winning him
over? Jenny is special. I think she could
be the one. It's just that we come from
different backgrounds and I don't want to
do anything to screw this up.
     Brand

He left the Internet program open and continued to labor over his
homework. He had a paper due next week, and he'd been agonizing over it
for the better part of the past month. It was time he got it finished.

He was surprised at how easily the words came. Maybe he did work
better when he was trying to put other things out of his mind.

It was almost midnight when he wrote the last word of the paper and
he heard the familiar ding indicating he'd received e-mail.

     Hey Brand
     Great to hear from you. If Jenny is as
important to you as you make her sound,
you'll find a way to win over her family.
Starting with her brother is a good idea. I
know I met David's sister Melanie first and
she was a great help. The younger
generation isn't as hung up on differences
as the older ones. His parents gave me a
little grief, but not as much as Grandma
and Grandpa Chi. Of course, now they think
I'm the best thing since sliced bread.
     Keep me posted on how things go this
weekend. I'm betting you'll be a hit with
the brother. It sounds like you're already
tops on Jenny's list. Just a side note,
little Mandy is growing like a weed and in

```
about   six   months   she'll   have   either   a
little  brother  or  sister.  Hopefully  you'll
be  able  to  make  it  out  to  see  us  in  the
near   future.   If   not,   I'll   see   you   at
Frannie's wedding.
   Cindy
```

Brand smiled at the note. Cindy had given up her dreams of being a lawyer to become a wife and mother, and the role suited her well. When he graduated, Brand hoped he'd have time to get out to San Francisco to spend a few days with Cindy and David.

After closing down the Internet and then the laptop, Brand went to bed. Cindy made him feel less uneasy about meeting Matt on Saturday. If he was anything like David's sister, Melanie, Brand was certain winning him over would be easy. At least he hoped so. He wanted Jenny in his life, but without her family's acceptance it would be a lot harder than anything he'd ever done in his life.

Chapter Four

Jenny picked out at least six different outfits before she decided on what to wear to meet her brother and Karen. She was glad Matt agreed to bring her along. It certainly made her situation with Brand easier to handle.

All her life her parents told her keeping her heritage was one of the most important things in her life. Brand wasn't part of her heritage, but she wanted him to be part of her life. Besides, it was only a college romance. Once they graduated in the spring, he would be going off to start his career. At the same time she would be returning to the reservation and the people who supported her dream. Without the scholarship from the doctors at the hospital, she would have never been able to get the education to return and help her people.

"Have you decided what to wear today?" Frannie looked up from the book she was reading.

"I guess so. What do you think of this?" Jenny held up the jeans she'd picked up at the resale shop last week, along with the matching jacket and the red print button down shirt.

"I thought the last five outfits were perfect too. I like this one, though. The red is a perfect color for you and you look great in those jeans. I agree with the jacket as well, since it's supposed to be cool today."

Jenny agreed. Just looking out the window of her dorm, she could study the tree-lined shore of the opposite side of the lake. The leaves were beginning to turn color, promising that soon they would leave the trees bare and winter would be settling in place. The clear blue October sky, combined with the weather forecast for today, told her the temperature would be crisp and cool.

She'd just finished putting on her jeans and shirt when someone knocked at the door. Frannie answered it while Jenny grabbed her jacket.

Brand entered the room and glanced at the bed filled with discarded clothes. "You look hot," he commented, as he crossed the room to give her a kiss on the cheek. "Fortunately, you would have looked great in any one of these outfits." He pointed to the clothes littering her bed.

"Okay, Mr. Smarty," Frannie said, "how many times did you change clothes before you decided what you should wear?"

"Unfair question," Brand replied with a wink. "You know me too well."

Jenny looked up at Brand. "Are you as nervous about today as I am?"

"Twice as much. You're not the one who's going to be under the microscope. I'm worried about what your brother will think of me."

Jenny laughed. "And I'm worried about what Karen will think about me. I know she makes him happy, but what if she decides she isn't quite as comfortable with the color of his skin once she realizes his entire family is different from anyone she's ever known?"

"Is that how you feel about my family?"

Brand's question caught her off guard. "You know it isn't. What you don't understand is it's different for a Native American in the white world. We're the minority and have learned to live with it. How will she feel when she's the only white person in a Native American family? It's always been that way."

Brand pulled her into his warm embrace. "I hope Karen is like me and is more tolerant of the differences. Being Native American sets you apart. The fact you're different is one of the reasons I was attracted to you. It isn't skin color that makes a person special. It's their personality that draws people to them. I couldn't love you if it wasn't for the fact you're the most special person I've ever met."

The word love reverberated in Jenny's mind. Over the past few weeks she'd secretly been falling in love with Brand, but to hear him say the same thing about her made her heart skip a beat. He loved her now, for the moment, but what would happen once they graduated and went their separate ways?

The warmth of the day came as a surprise considering Thanksgiving was only a little over a month away. Jenny wore the jacket she'd picked out, not for warmth, but for fashion. The short walk to the Memorial Union was pleasant. They weren't the only ones out walking. It seemed as though every student on campus was enjoying the last warm weather of the season by riding bikes in the bike lanes of the main streets, walking on the sidewalks, or roller blading in the park as well as along the lakefront.

"Matt couldn't have chosen a better weekend to come to Madison," Jenny observed.

"I'll say. What do you think he'll want to do?"

"The first thing will be to go out to eat. I had an e-mail from him last night, and he said he'll have his car and wants to check out The Melting Pot."

"I've been thinking of going there," Brand said. "There just hasn't been time. I remember my folks telling about how they used to have fondue parties when they were first married. My dad said he liked the ones with either meatballs or steak since Mom used to make all kinds of dips to go with them. As I recall, his favorite was sour cream and horseradish. Mom has always been a chocoholic. She said she really liked dipping strawberries into the hot chocolate."

"From what I hear it's really expensive. Matt said he received a gift certificate from a client and decided to treat us today. I'm really looking forward to it. I went online and checked out their menu. Everything sounds wonderful, and I'm planning to enjoy every bite of it."

Matt and Karen were just pulling into the parking lot when Jenny and Brand arrived. After the introductions, they got into Matt's car for the short ride to the Melting Pot on Odana Road. While Matt and Karen occupied the front seat, Brand and Jenny got into the cramped back seat of the compact car.

"So how long have you known my sister," Matt asked.

"We met on the day she moved into the dorm. I'm her upstairs neighbor. She's my sister's roommate, and my roommate is engaged to my sister. We got together out of desperation in order to get out of being alone every night that either of us have free."

"Kinda sounds like Matt and me," Karen said. "I ended up renting an apartment in his building, and the first day I was there, I sorta commandeered his parking space with the big truck my dad rented to help me move in my stuff. He was mad as a wet hen when he had to park out on the street. By the time he came storming into the lobby, I was just coming out for another load. I honestly thought he was going to go on the warpath and scalp me."

The thought of her brother wearing war paint and a three-piece suit, getting ready to use a scalping knife made Jenny laugh hysterically.

"It's not that funny, Jen," Matt protested. "I don't think anyone's recorded a scalping by a Chippewa brave in over a hundred years. For that matter, I doubt the Chippewa even knew how to use a scalping knife. From all the stories I've ever heard, we were always a peaceful people."

"So far, I've found Jennifer is peaceful, but then I've been very careful not to make her angry," Brand responded.

Jenny turned to Brand. "I thought you were supposed to be my boyfriend."

"I am. I guess I just got caught up in the mental picture of Indians on the warpath."

"Get used to it, Jen," Matt said. "I hear things like this a lot from the white eyes I work with. Even so, I'm not giving up on Karen just because of her warped opinion of this noble savage."

"I'll give you noble," Jenny replied, "but I think I'll pass on the savage part. As I recall, you and Dad always went to a cabin when you were out hunting. Mom said it had something to do with not having indoor plumbing and soft beds in the tent that Uncle Mike liked to use."

"You didn't tell me that," Karen teased. "When you said you went deer hunting with your dad, I envisioned you roughing it the same way my dad and brothers do."

The good-natured teasing ended when Matt parked the car in the restaurant's lot.

"Have either of you ever been here?" Karen said when they entered the lobby.

"We were talking about that earlier," Brand replied. "On a student's budget we usually don't splurge on such an extravagant place. We're more comfortable eating in the hospital cafeteria, since that's where we spend most of our time, and they give us a good discount."

"I hear you there," Matt said. "Even though I'm making good money now, I still remember what it was like to be a struggling student. I usually don't go to places like this, but since my client gave me a gift certificate, I decided to share it with Karen and my favorite college student sister."

"I'm your only college student sister, at least the only one in Madison, you jerk. It doesn't matter. I looked up the menu on line, and I'm looking forward to Wisconsin Trio cheese fondue, a California salad, and an amaretto meltdown for dessert."

"I looked up the menu, too," Karen added. "I'm leaning toward the cheddar cheese with the yin and yang and a mushroom salad."

"What's this, a mutiny?" Brand said. "Don't we get a choice?"

"Sure we do," Matt teased. "You've been a student far too long. Once you get into the outside world, you'll find out that whatever your girlfriend wants is exactly what you want. It saves a lot of fights. Besides I've had both of those cheese fondues and the desserts, and it's a toss-up as to which one is the best. I personally like the chef's salad, but that's nothing more than personal preference. I think the girls have made excellent choices."

They all enjoyed a good laugh as the hostess escorted them to their table. Once they were seated and their orders taken, Matt took Karen's hand in his.

"This morning when we were driving down here, I asked Karen a very important question. She said she wouldn't give me an answer until she met you."

Jenny looked into Karen's eyes. In them she could see love for Matt. If he'd asked her to marry him, would she say yes? Jenny certainly hoped so.

"If Jenny is any indication of what the rest of your family is like, I'd be proud to be your wife."

Jenny watched, with only a hint of jealousy, as Matt took Karen in his arms and kissed her tenderly. Once they broke the embrace, he reached into his pocket and produced a ring box containing a beautiful marquis cut diamond ring.

She thought of all the promises Charlie had made to her when he wanted to take her to bed for the first time. There had been words of love mingled with how one day they would be married and start a family.

Instead, they started the family, and he said he wanted nothing to do with either her or his son.

Not wanting to put a damper on Matt's joyous news, she bit back her tears and smiled at her brother and her soon to be sister-in-law.

* * * *

Brand watched Jenny's reaction to Matt's proposal and Karen's acceptance. As soon as Matt mentioned asking Karen an important question, Brand thought it was a marriage proposal. He hoped Karen would say yes and open the door for him and Jenny to become more than just a dating couple. Before graduation in June, he hoped to ask her to marry him. If her family willingly accepted Karen, it would make things much easier for him.

Once Karen gave Matt her answer, Brand got to his feet. "This calls for a toast," he said, raising his water glass. "To Karen and Matt. May you have a wonderful life together."

"Here, here," came the echoed response from several of the other diners. To his surprise, they were also on their feet with water glasses raised in salute of Matt and Karen."

Matt beamed at the congratulations, while Karen blushed. "Thank you one and all," Matt said, pulling Karen into a tight embrace and kissing her passionately.

Brand turned to Jenny to see how she was responding to her brother's spontaneity. Instead of the smile he expected, he saw tears in her eyes.

"What's wrong?" he whispered.

Jenny wiped her eyes with her napkin. "Nothing, it's just that Matt has always been my big brother. I'm so happy for him, but at the same time I don't want to share him, not even with the love of his life."

"Never fear, Little One, I'll always be your big brother," Matt said, as the waiter brought them their fondue and salads.

They had just begun to eat when the hostess came to their table with a bottle of wine. "The manager said that if you were going to toast the announcement of your engagement he wants you to do it with a good wine rather than water. It's compliments of the management."

Brand was impressed at how good the wine actually tasted. He did notice Jenny didn't drink much. He knew she usually didn't drink, but this was a special occasion.

* * * *

Jenny knew she's been less than truthful when she said she worried about losing her brother. The most worrying to her was how her parents would react to Karen being white.

Her father served on the council of elders and preached constantly about keeping their blood pure and not intermarrying with the whites. She prayed they would be able to look beyond the ethnic differences between Matt and Karen and see the love radiating from their eyes. It was the same look she saw exchanged between her parents her entire life. She'd always wanted that kind of love when she found someone special.

As soon as the thought crossed her mind, she glanced at Brand. He made her feel not only loved, but also certain he wanted to become special in her life.

"If it makes you feel any better, Jen, Karen's father is a quarter Cherokee."

Jen looked skeptically at Karen's blonde hair and sky blue eyes. "Cherokee?"

"I know my hair and eyes don't look like it," Karen said, "but trust me, it's true. I take after my mom. She's one hundred percent Norwegian. Both her parents came from there prior to World War II. They came from a small community in Minnesota where Mom married the son of the farmer down the road. His parents were also from Norway. Guess the blue eyes and blonde hair turned out to be the more dominant gene. Now when you meet my brother, you'd swear that he was a throwback. As a matter of fact, he belongs to a drum group, and they travel around the country during the summer performing at pow-wows."

"Doesn't he work," Brand asked.

"He runs a computer based business from home. He's pretty much free to set his own schedule. It works well, especially because he enjoys the pow-wows."

Jenny watched Brand intently. She was positive he had never been to a pow-wow in his life. It was a shame, since he had no idea what he was missing.

"You should have come home with me last summer like I wanted you to, Karen," Matt said. "We had a great pow-wow. Jenny looked great and her little guy, Alex, danced like a pro. I'm sure he'd been practicing for weeks."

"You have a son?" Karen said.

Jenny suddenly became uncomfortable with the conversation. Even though Brand knew about Alex she certainly didn't want to throw it in his face at every turn.

"You bet she does," Brand answered before she had a chance to say anything. "I've seen the pictures, and he looks like a great kid. I can hardly wait to meet him."

Like that's ever going to happen. Mom and Dad would have a fit if they knew she was dating a white guy who had absolutely no Native American blood. He talked a good show, but she knew once they graduated and went their separate ways, she'd be nothing more than a pleasant memory. She wanted it to be more, yet knew she wouldn't curl up and die when the break-up happened. She'd make the most of this year and have wonderful memories to keep her warm once she went home and became a real mother to her son.

"Did you hear me, Jen?" Matt had a hint of irritation in his voice.

"I'm sorry; I guess my mind was wandering. What did you say?"

"I asked if you had any pictures of the little prince in your purse."

"Now that's a silly question. Of course I do. Mom sent me the new school pictures last week."

She reached into her purse and brought out her wallet with the new school picture on the opposite side of the plastic pocket from her driver's license.

"Oh, he's adorable. How old is he," Karen asked.

"He's five. This is his first year at school. From the e-mails Mom sends, it sounds like he's doing very well. I really hate missing all these firsts in his life, but after this year I'll be able to become a full time mom."

"Do you already have a job lined up?"

"Better than that," Matt replied before Jenny could answer. "The hospital gave her a full scholarship with the stipulation that she return after graduation and take a position there. Knowing my sister, she'll be running the joint in a couple of years."

The conversation continued all through lunch, but Jenny's mind was elsewhere. All her life she had envisioned herself working at the hospital, and now she was having second thoughts. Seeing her brother so happy with a woman whose skin wasn't the same color as his and with blonde hair made her wish she could share the same kind of happiness with Brand. Of course, it was nothing more than a pipe dream. She had a life on the reservation with a top job as well as a son who loved her with all his heart.

On the day she gave birth, she gave up all dreams of love, at least love in the same way Matt and Karen knew it. She had her son to think about, and nothing else mattered. Maybe when he was grown and on his own, she could think of such things, but not now.

Chapter Five

Thanksgiving vacation was only hours away. Jenny's last class was at eight on Wednesday morning, and she had her car packed for the trip home. By leaving as soon as the class was finished, she could be home by the time Alex came home from school. It was hard for her to believe they actually made five-year-old kids go to school all day, but her mother assured her Alex loved every minute of his days at school.

"Are you all packed?"

She turned to see Brand standing in the doorway. "I just have to take this bag down to the car. How about you?"

"I'm driving Frannie and me back home as soon as her last class is over. I'm looking forward to having an entire weekend without being on call. Poor Greg, he'll be working Thanksgiving, so he'll have to be content with the turnkey they serve in the cafeteria. At least when I'm out on my own, the hours will be better. That said, I'll also have to work my shifts at the hospital like everyone else."

Jenny laughed at his comment. "Like you'll be working in a hospital. I can see you in private practice being on call, but not likely having to spend your holidays in the hospital at all."

"A lot you know. Anyway, if we stand here talking much longer, you'll be late for class. I'll see you on Monday morning, unless you get back earlier and then it's possible I'll see you on Sunday."

"Oh Brand, that's the sweetest thing you could say to me, but I don't want to miss a minute I can have with Alex. I've missed him terribly, and this is the first chance I've had to get home since school started in September."

He pulled her into an embrace and kissed her with what could almost be called urgency. His kiss brought her warring emotions to the forefront. Her first and most important priority was Alex. Her son needed her. What about her needs? She knew the internal question was a mute point. As long as she had a son who needed her, the needs and wants of a healthy young woman had to come second.

Even though Brand made overtures toward her now, everything would change once they both graduated in June. He would be a young white doctor with a promising future. She would be a single mother and Chippewa woman to boot. The hospital on the reservation had paid for her education, and she owed her allegiance to them. It didn't matter that she wanted to be special to Brand because to do so she would have to leave her people, the very people who had funded her education, and move far away from her home. There was no way she could take her son away from the grandparents who raised him or the legacy of the heritage to which he was entitled.

"I'll see you on Monday," she said.

The voice of reason made sense. She would spend as much time as possible with Alex and come back to Madison in time for class on Monday.

* * * *

Jenny didn't think her morning class would ever end. Although it lasted no longer than usual, she thought the time dragged. It was after nine before she was on the road and heading north.

From the campus, she took East Washington to Highway 51 and followed it all the way to Woodruff where she took Highway 47 the rest of the way home. Stopping only for gas, she arrived at the elementary school by three thirty when Alex was dismissed for the day. Once she knew she was going to make it, she placed a call to her mother so she wouldn't go to the school.

As she waited for the dismissal bell, Jenny thought about what it was like to be a student here. Back then, her future shone brightly, and she could have done anything with her life. At one point, she wanted to be a doctor, but reality set in when she realized how long it would take her to finish the schooling necessary to receive the coveted degree. Then, her dream changed, and she wanted to become a nurse.

The teachers who trained her made her grateful for their patience. She also gave thanks to the doctors at the hospital who arranged for her to receive the scholarship that enabled her to go to the UW.

The sound of the bell ringing brought her back from the memories of the past to the reality that in a few short minutes she would hold her son in her arms and be with him for the next four days.

Children ran out of the school, waving pictures of turkeys and wearing headbands with feathers to indicate they were the Indians who had helped the Pilgrims for the first Thanksgiving.

"Mommy, Mommy, I knew you'd be here," Alex called as he opened the passenger door of her car and reached across the seat to hug her tightly. "Grandma said you'd be here."

"I was lucky the roads were good, and I didn't hit a lot of traffic. How was your day at school?"

"Oh, Mommy, we learned the Indians brought food to the Pilgrims for the first Thanksgiving. We had a feast for lunch, and I got to be an Indian. The first graders were the Pilgrims, and we served them corn and venison."

Jenny smiled as she listened to Alex describe the mock feast. She wondered if the white children who learned about the first Thanksgiving even knew what venison was. It was a shame. To them Thanksgiving was eating turkey and talking about the Pilgrims with no thought at all to the Indians who befriended them during the first years they were trying to make their home in a hostile land.

She waited for the traffic to thin before pulling away from the curb and heading toward her childhood home.

"I told my teacher you were coming home today, and she said she's going to call you to talk about me."

"Should I be worried about your teacher wanting to talk to me?" she teased.

"No Mommy," Alex replied, suddenly more sober than before. "She wants me to start reading, and she says she has to talk to you about it first. She tells me I'm one of her best students."

"I know you are, Sweetie. I was only teasing you."

It took only a few more minutes for them to drive the rest of the way home. At last they pulled into the familiar driveway where her mother waited on the porch.

"I'm so glad to have you home," Betsy exclaimed. "I've worried about you all day. I don't like you driving all that way by yourself."

"Well, Mama, this is the last year you'll have to worry. By this time next year, Alex and I will have our own place and be completely out of your hair."

"Oh dear, I hope not. Your father and I have been talking, and we're thinking about adding on to the house so you and Alex can have your own apartment."

"Thanks Mom, but there's no need for you to go to that expense. I'll be making enough money. I'll be able to rent a place for us. Besides, I'm counting on you to take care of Alex after school and when I have to work the weekends. You won't be getting rid of us entirely."

"Well, if this is what you want, I know of a nice little house that will be available about the same time you get out of school."

"You do? Where?"

Her mother glanced to her left. Her father purchased the little house next door to them several years ago and had been renting it out.

"How are you so sure your renters will be leaving?"

"They gave us notice last week. In the spring, they're building their own place. It's supposed to be ready for them to move in by the first of July. That means you'll only be staying with us for a month, six weeks at the most. You know the layout of the place, and you can decorate it any way you want. Our anniversary is next spring, and your father has promised me new living room and dining room furniture. If you want, we can give you our stuff for your house, at least until you can get something more to your liking."

"Are you sure about this?"

"Positive. We've been saving for a long time for a special twenty-fifth anniversary present. I've had my furniture picked out for months. We went to Woodruff last weekend and put it all on layaway. To be truthful, I was happy when Ruthie and John decided to build their own place. I wasn't looking forward to the remodel your father had planned for this

A Father's Love

winter so you could move in with us. You know how his projects go. If we had it done by June, it would be a miracle."

Jenny laughed at her mother's description of her father's efforts when it came to any kind of project. While her mother took Alex into the house for milk and cookies as an after school treat, Jenny studied the house next door. She had always loved the house. When she'd been a little girl, an older couple lived there. They were like another set of grandparents to her. When her mother was working, she would go there after school for the treats Alma baked. The kitchen would always remind her of freshly baked cookies and all the other goodies that came from Alma's oven.

"Did you hear me, Jenny?"

She shook off the memories of the past and turned toward her mother. "I'm sorry, Mom, I was thinking about Alma. I think living in her old house will be wonderful. I won't be far from you and Dad, and I won't have to worry about Alex, either."

"I'm glad you're receptive to our idea, but what I asked didn't have anything to do with the house. I was wondering if you've heard anything about this girl Matt says he's bringing home for Thanksgiving."

"Yes, I have. He brought her down to Madison at the end of October so we could meet. I liked her right off. Why do you ask?"

"I'm afraid he's very serious about her, and I worry about her being white."

"Things are changing, Mom. Karen is white, but her father is a quarter Cherokee. To answer your question, he is serious about her. I think it's great. They make a perfect couple. I just think I should warn you, though, she is very blonde."

"How can that be? If her father has Cherokee blood, how can she be blonde?"

"Her mother's family is Norwegian. She takes after her mother, but she assures me that her brother could easily pass for Cherokee."

"I guess I'll just have to reserve judgment until I meet her. Now, what about you? I don't like the fact you're not dating, or are you and just not telling us?"

"I'm seeing someone. It's not serious. He's a medical student and the brother of my roommate. His name is Brand Masterson."

41

She cringed at the white lie she just told. It would be easy for her to consider spending her life with Brand, but she knew the differences in their backgrounds as well as their goals would make it completely impossible.

"I take it he's white."

"Yes Mother, he's white. We get along very well. Of course, we don't get to see a lot of each other, except when he has a few days off. He's in his last year of residency and very busy at the hospital. He works, sometimes thirty hours at a stretch, so most of his free time is spent sleeping."

"Thirty hours at a time, how can they do that to those students?"

"Brand says it's part of becoming a doctor. He says everyone has to pay their dues. I'm just glad I don't have to put in those long hours to become a nurse."

"I agree. So when do we get to meet your young man?"

"Probably never. He has Thanksgiving off, but that means he'll have to work on Christmas as well as on New Year's."

"Then why didn't you invite him to spend Thanksgiving with us?"

"You know as well as I do that Dad would throw a fit about him being white. Besides, he's spending the holiday with his family in Pinehurst. Of course, once he finishes his schooling in June, he'll be off to work in some big hospital in one of the major cities. His roommate tells me Brand is one of the best doctors in their class."

"You aren't fooling me Jennifer Marie Red Hawk. You're in love with him and trying not to show it. I understand how it is when you've had your heart broken once, but the thing with Charlie is over and done with. As soon as your schooling is finished, you should start thinking about settling down. Alex needs a father to say nothing of brothers and sisters."

"I'm afraid your kind of happily ever after is not in the picture for me. I'm committed to the hospital here and that means there won't be much time for either romance or babies."

Her mother's exasperated sigh told Jenny she wanted to see her daughter settled and happy rather than working her tail off at the hospital.

* * * *

42

A Father's Love

Brand watched as Jenny drove off. His holiday started last night and would be over on Monday morning. He knew he should have left early, but he didn't want to miss any time with Jenny. Besides, he had to wait until Frannie finished the last of her classes this morning. The two of them decided to drive home together to save on gas. With the price of gas going up, driving anywhere separately became too expensive.

He waited until Jenny turned the corner before going back in to finish packing his duffel for the weekend at home. He smiled to think Jenny wasn't planning to come back to Madison until Monday. He'd have to talk to Frannie. Since Greg didn't get the weekend off, he knew she wanted to come back to Madison on Friday night in order to spend any time possible with him. If she did, maybe he could talk her into making a detour. He hoped the folks would understand him wanting to spend some of his free time with Jenny over the weekend.

He'd been e-mailing her brother Matt about the possibility of him coming to the reservation to meet the family. At first, Matt had been cautious about it, but finally said if he planned to spring Karen on the family over the holiday, maybe Brand should plan on meeting them as well.

"Are you ready to leave?" Frannie said as she entered his room without knocking.

"You're lucky I wasn't standing here in the altogether."

"I knew you wouldn't be. I saw you telling Jenny good-bye. It's a shame the two of you can't spend some of your off time together."

"That's want I wanted to talk to you about. I just got off the phone with Mom and Dad and talked it over with them. If you're willing to make a slight detour on the way back to campus, I will be spending time with Jenny."

"What are you getting at?"

"I know you're coming back on Friday, so if I could hitch a ride to the reservation, I've made arrangements with Jenny's brother, Matt, to meet him at the community center. I have his cell number, so I can call when we get there."

"Are you sure that's such a good idea? Jenny is really paranoid about what her family will think of her dating a white guy. Besides, there's Alex to consider. She's his mother and—"

"And that's all the more reason for me to go to the reservation on Friday. I want to get to know this kid. She's working her tail off to give him a good life. A life, I might add, that I want to be a part of. I'm hoping Matt's engagement to Karen will grease the way for me to get into her parents' good graces."

"Well, it will be your butt on the line. If they don't like you, it could be a very long weekend."

Brand agreed. It wouldn't be easy winning over Jenny's folks, but he had to try. If he wanted her in his life once they graduated, he had to make a good case to her parents.

Chapter Six

Jenny checked over all the pictures Alex had drawn in school for the past three months. To her amazement, he wasn't a bad artist. She only had one or two of them she had to ask him what they were. The last thing he showed her was a book he'd written.

My name is Alex. My mommy is Jenny. She goes to school.

A picture he drew accompanied each statement. The first one was a little boy with coppery skin. The second was a woman, supposedly herself, holding the hand of the little boy at her side. Lastly, there was a picture of a square building that looked like the grade school, with a big red UW on the front of it.

"Very impressive," she mused, more to herself than to Alex.

"Grandma told me what color to make the letters. I wish you didn't have ta go to school, Mommy."

Jenny pulled him into her arms. Because of her school, she missed his first day of school and even the loss of his first tooth. "Me too, Alex, but after I graduate, I'll be back here all the time, and you'll get tired of having me around. We're going to live in the house next door to Grandma and Grandpa, and together we'll decide how to decorate it."

"Can I have my room any way I want?"

"That's right, any way you want. How would you like it?"

"I don't know, maybe Spiderman or Cars. I like both of those movies. Grandpa taked me to see both of them."

"He took you, Alex, not taked. Anyway once I'm done with school we'll go to lots of movies together."

Alex looked at her skeptically. "I don't think so, Mommy. Grandpa lets me have popcorn and soda and candy. When we take Grandma, she tells me not to eat any junk food. Grandpa and I tell her it's 'our man time' when we go to the movies and girls can't go. That way we can eat all the stuff from the food counter and no one yells at us."

"Oh, I see. Well, I can understand why you need 'man time' with your Grandpa. I can remember when he used to take me and your aunt and uncles to the movies. We didn't want Grandma to come along either, mainly because she wouldn't let us get all the goodies we liked to eat."

Alex hugged her tightly. "Grandpa said you'd say that. I love you, Mommy."

The sound of the door closing, caused him to slide down off her lap and run into the living room calling out her youngest brother, Doug's name.

Jenny put all of Alex's treasures back into the shoebox he used for them and headed toward the living room to see her brother. This would be his last year of high school and he was still trying to decide where to go to school in the fall. He'd been offered a scholarship to play football for the University of Wisconsin in Madison as well as one from Marquette.

"Hey, Sis, when did you get in?" Doug said as soon as she entered the room.

"I drove like the devil to be here in time for Alex to get out of school. How about you? Any idea of where you're going to school in the fall?"

"I know the folks are pushing for me to go to UW, but I'm leaning toward Marquette. I know Matt went to Platteville, you're at Madison, and Les is at Eau Claire, but I like what Marquette is offering better. I especially like their pre-law program. For now, I'm leaning toward being a lawyer. I figure if I take up law, you become a nurse, Les is a teacher, and Matt continues in architecture, we'll have everything in the family covered."

Jenny laughed. Matt enjoyed his position with the architectural firm in Appleton, she would soon have her nursing degree, and Leslie would be graduating in two years with a degree in teaching. All together, they were living the dream that her parents had had for them all their lives.

46

A Father's Love

"Do you know when Les is planning to get here," Jenny asked.

"She told Mom she wouldn't be in until late tonight. She has a late class. If you ask me, it's not a class that's keeping her after school. I think she has a boyfriend. I keep telling her, she's not at school to be a party girl, but she says it's the only chance she's going to get. There're not a lot of eligible guys around here."

"Are Mom and Dad upset about her dating?"

"They don't say much. You know how they are. I think they're more upset about this girl Matt is bringing home. They think she's white."

Jenny nodded her head. "I know. Mom and I talked about it when I first got here. Karen is white, but her father is one-quarter Cherokee. That has to count for something. I've met her, and she's great. I'm betting the folks will like her as well."

"Jen, can you help me in the kitchen?" Their mother's question ended Jenny and her brother's conversation.

* * * *

"We're home," Brand called when they entered the house. "Is anyone here?"

"I'm out in the kitchen," his mother's voice answered.

Brand hurried to where his mother was busy making soup for supper. On the counter, he saw the array of pies and bars for Thanksgiving dinner.

"How long will we be graced with the honor of your presence this year?" His mother gave him a hug, then turned to hug Frannie.

"Greg has to work this weekend, so I'm going back Friday morning to be at least in the same city as him. We're planning an elaborate Thanksgiving feast at the hospital cafeteria on Saturday."

"And I'm going back with her. You see there's this girl…"

"You don't have to say anymore. Frannie has been going on and on about her roommate and that the two of you are an item. Besides, your father told me about your plans to go to the reservation on Friday to meet her folks. Did Jenny's parents invite you to spend the remainder of the weekend with them?"

"Not really. I'm going to be a bit of a surprise to everyone but her brother. He knows I'm coming. He said he'd make reservations for me at a motel. I'm not sure how they'll react to me. I'm not even sure how Jenny will react. It's a mixed cultural thing."

"How can they help but like you? Anyway, why don't you children get the table set? Your father will be here soon and ready to eat."

Brand helped Frannie set the table. When he set foot in this house, it was as though he entered a time warp and went to when he was still in high school and Frannie was in middle school. Back then, it was always their job to not only set the table but also to clear it and take care of the dishes. At least here, some things never changed.

It surprised Brand to realize his parents weren't overly disturbed by his decision to leave on Friday when Frannie went back to Madison. He decided they were used to being on their own and having grown children return home for any length of time was an imposition on their happy empty nest.

"When will Suzie be getting here?" Frannie said as they helped their mother clear the table.

"They'll be getting in later tonight. She had to work all day, and of course, then there's the drive from Rockford. Ron said he'd have the car all packed and be ready to leave with the kids as soon as she got out of work."

It excited Brand to think his older sister would be arriving tonight. He wanted to talk to her about Jenny. "That's good, because I want to talk to her."

"Oh really," his father said. "The two of you usually don't have a lot to talk about."

"Well, we do now. I guess it's time I told you more about Jenny. I really think she's the one."

"The one?" his father said.

"That's right. I just have to convince her as well as her parents that I want her in my life. She has some baggage I think you ought to know about. She got pregnant before her junior year in high school, just like Suzie did. The difference is she kept her son. Her parents are helping her raise him until she can get back to work at the hospital on the reservation and make a good life for the two of them."

"What about the child's father," his mother asked.

48

"He's not in the picture. From what Jenny says, he's never even seen the boy. The reason I'm having Frannie take me to the reservation on Friday is so I can meet the boy as well as her parents."

"I don't know what your sister can tell you," his father said, shaking his head. "She's in an entirely different position."

"Well, not really. She had to tell Ron about Michael. It's true she doesn't have custody of him, but it was something he had to know. She didn't want there to be any secrets in their relationship. As for Jenny, she told me about Alex the first day we met. I think it was possible she thought I would turn away from her once I knew the truth. The way she tells it, things haven't been easy for her. You know how cruel kids can be, and she continued to go to high school after Alex was born, plus she's been working her tail off going to school to become a nurse."

Both his parents nodded their agreement with his need to know how hard things had been for Suzie and Ron when it came to the knowledge that Suzie had had a baby before she was old enough to be a mother.

By eight-thirty, the table was cleared and the dishes were done. They'd just settled down to watch television, but Brand wasn't interested in the program his father insisted on watching. Since the old man found TruTV, it seemed all he wanted to watch were the police shows they ran. Instead of becoming involved in the program, Brand thumbed through the latest issue of National Geographic while he waited for Suzie and Ron to arrive.

"We're home," Suzie called as she came into the house with husband and kids in tow.

It always amazed him at how fast the children grew since the last time he'd seen them. Adrian was now eight and Zack six. Once they'd started school, they seemed to grow quicker than they had before.

Adrian was the first to get to Brand and demand her usual hug and a kiss, followed closely by her younger brother. "Mommy said you'd be here. There's snow outside, do you think we can go sledding tomorrow morning?" Zack said.

The thought of frogging around in the snow on Thanksgiving morning was something Brand looked forward to doing. He never denied his niece and nephew anything to make them happy. If they were going to go sledding at all, it would have to be tomorrow, because he was planning to leave early on Friday morning to get to the reservation.

"Sounds like a plan. Maybe we can persuade your Aunt Frannie to join us."

"Oh no you don't," Frannie protested. "I don't do cold, remember?"

"It will be good practice for you. Once you and Greg get married, I don't think you'll wait too long to bring more little munchkins into the world. We can go sledding on the hill behind the house early tomorrow morning and work up an appetite for Mom's great lunch."

Frannie threw up her hands in mock surrender. "All right, it looks like I'm outnumbered. Just remember this. When my little munchkins come you'd better be ready to go sledding with them as well."

Brand chuckled as Frannie continued to fume. He knew it was all a show, but she enjoyed it nonetheless. It took Suzie and Ron several minutes to get the kids settled down and into bed. Once they returned to the living room, her mother brought them roast beef sandwiches from the dinner leftovers.

Suzie sat down next to Brand on the couch to eat her supper. "Do you mind if I ask you and Ron a personal question," Brand asked.

"This sounds serious," Suzie replied.

"It is," Frannie replied before Brand could say a word. "You see, he's met a girl, and she has a five year old son. He wants them both in his life, and he's wondering how you broke the news to Ron about Michael."

"If she hasn't told you about the boy, how do you know about him?" Suzie said.

"That was the first thing she told me," Brand responded, annoyed with Frannie for blurting everything out without giving him a chance to answer for himself.

"If you already know about him, I don't see how I can help. It sounds like she's raising the boy. Does it bother you? Do you wish she'd put him up for adoption like I did with Michael?"

"Good grief no, to both questions. I'm just worried that she doesn't want me to be in the boy's life. I've fallen in love with her, and I think she has the same feelings for me. It's just that she's Chippewa, and her family might not be too happy with me seeing their daughter. There's another problem, one I hope to rectify this weekend, but it's still a problem. She is planning to work in the hospital on the Lac du Flambeau Reservation when she finishes school. I'm thinking of applying at the hospital there. I doubt being Chippewa is a prerequisite for doctors."

"Again, I don't know how I can help you. Since you know about the boy, and her being a mother doesn't bother you, I don't see any problem in that department. Now her parents could be something else altogether. If you're planning to go to the reservation this weekend, I'm sure you'll win them over."

"I certainly hope so. A couple of weeks ago I met her brother. He came to Madison to get Jenny's approval of his fiancé. She's white, and he was worried about what their parents would say. The difference is her father has a Native American heritage and I don't. If they don't approve of her, what will they say about me?"

"You're on your own on this one, Little Brother. I don't think I have any great words of wisdom for you."

Brand nodded. There was nothing anyone in his family could do to help him. It was something he was going to have to work out for himself.

* * * *

Jenny helped her mother fix Thanksgiving dinner. As usual, relatives would filled the house. Her father's brother, Sam, and his family would be coming along with Grandma and Grandpa Red Hawk, as well as Clayton and Alice Straight Arrow. Even Doug was bringing a date. She, along with her cousins Judy and Jean, would be the only singles at the table since their brother, Josh, had married the love of his life, Cathy Little Horse, Charlie's younger sister, last year. In total, there would be eighteen people to devour her mother's twenty-five pound turkey.

The dinner guests began arriving at precisely eleven. Aunt Regina brought her sweet potato pie, while Judy brought a large salad, and Jean a pan of apple slices to go along with the pumpkin pies Grandma Red Hawk made. Alice Straight Arrow from next door brought a large basket of rolls. Added to the potatoes, stuffing, and corn, Jenny helped prepare the cranberry relish Karen insisted was one of her specialties added to the remainder of the meal.

Once they were all enjoying their dessert, her father got to his feet. "Today is, indeed a day for great announcements," he began. "I will start by saying this summer, Betsy and I are planning our first vacation in years. We're going to take an Alaskan cruise."

The announcement took Jenny by complete surprise. Her parents never took a vacation, to say nothing of going on a cruise. She knew they'd been saving since their twenty-fifth anniversary for the furniture her mother wanted, but this was something she hadn't expected.

"As I recall, we went to your twenty-fifth party a couple of years ago, big brother," Uncle Sam said.

"That was when we got the idea," Tom replied. "We put away the money we got from the party and continued to add to it until we could afford to go first class all the way. It's what Betsy deserves."

Jenny silently applauded her father. She knew he loved her mother with all his heart and what he now said made it perfectly clear to everyone at the table.

Matt also got to his feet, "Well, in July, Karen and I will be getting married. You're all invited to the wedding in Appleton. We're looking into hotel accommodations for everyone."

Congratulations resounded around the table. For Jenny, it was like a beginning. If her family accepted Karen, maybe, just maybe, she would be able to raise the subject of Brand before she returned to school on Sunday.

Doug also made an announcement. "After graduation, I'll be going to Marquette in Milwaukee. They've offered me a great scholarship, and I've accepted it. I'm planning to study law."

"That makes us next," Josh said. "We told the folks and Cathy's parents last month, before her mom and dad left for Florida. By the time they got back, her Mom had bought out half the baby stores in Tampa. We're going to have a baby in June. It will be her folk's first grandchild."

Josh's words cut Jenny to the quick. Her euphoria over Matt's announcement was suddenly crushed. She always thought Cathy knew about Alex being Charlie's child, his parent's first grandchild. Now it was evident even though Ben had helped her to support her son, he kept his relationship with Alex a secret from the rest of the family. The bitter thoughts crowding her mind moved to her stomach and made her want nothing more than to be alone.

"What about you, Jen," her father asked. "Don't you have an announcement to make?"

A Father's Love

More than anything else, she wanted to say she'd met a wonderful man who was white, but she didn't dare. Instead, she got to her feet swallowing the words burning on her tongue, and donned a false smile.

"I'll be graduating in June and retuning here to practice nursing. I should be home in time for Doug's graduation party. Thanks to Mom and Dad, I'll even have my own house. I'm thrilled about Clayton and Alice moving into a place of their own. I'm going to be taking over the rental of their house. I'll be close enough to home so Mom can watch Alex before and after school and during the summer, but far enough away to be completely on my own."

"You don't have to worry about a babysitter while your folks are on vacation," Sarah Eagle, Doug's current girlfriend, said. "Between Doug and me, we're planning to take over those duties for you. Neither of us will be leaving for college until fall so our entire summer will be free."

Jenny smiled, halfheartedly, at the offer. She knew Sarah was planning to get her teaching degree and was going to school in Milwaukee in order to be close to Doug. She couldn't help but wonder if they would return to the reservation once they finished their educations. Everyone she knew made the same promise when they went away to school, but few actually kept it. Like so many others, Charlie was God only knew where, and Matt was in Appleton. She wondered if she was a fool to consider coming back to work at the hospital here instead of following Brand to whatever hospital he picked.

As usual, the men took over the duties of clearing the table and doing the dishes while the women stayed in the living room to relax.

Once they were alone, the talk was about wedding, babies, and vacations. For the first time in her life, Jenny felt like an outsider. During her pregnancy with Ben Little Horse's first grandchild, it stayed a well-guarded secret. Now it was something even his Aunt Cathy didn't know.

Suddenly the room seemed too small, the air too stale for Jenny to stay any longer. "I'm sorry. I have a terrible headache. I'm going up to my room and lie down for a while."

Everyone looked at her strangely, but she left the room rather than stay and listen to the excited plans of her family and friends. There were just some things that were too difficult sit through, and these topics ranked at the top of the list. If it weren't for Alex, she would pack her bags and return to Madison tonight.

Instead, she closed the door and put the hook into the eye assuring her privacy. When she was certain she wouldn't be disturbed, she lay on her bed and cried all the bitter tears she refused to shed for years because she didn't want to upset Alex. For her, there would be no happily ever after, because her parents would never accept the man she had come to love over the past months. Brand would have a good life, and she would have to be content as a single mother working her daily shifts at the hospital to support her son.

Chapter Seven

Jenny was happy her parents accepted Matt and Karen marrying. Just as she told Matt, they liked Karen and because of her Native American heritage welcomed her into the family.

Their acceptance of Karen made Jenny's heart ache. Since yesterday, she had known they would never accept Brand as readily. During her time alone in her room yesterday afternoon, she had come to grips with her situation. Brand was as far from Native American as anyone could get. Frannie told her they were a combination of English and Swedish. There was no way she could ever bring him home to meet her parents.

Besides, once they graduated in the spring, he would be off to some big hospital in one of the large cities, and she would be here working at the local hospital. It wasn't anything she minded. This was where she belonged. She couldn't see herself working in a strange city and treating people who were so very different from her.

"A penny for your thoughts, Sis," Matt said, putting his arm around her shoulder.

"I was just thinking about how happy you and Karen are going to be."

"Who says you and Brand couldn't be this happy? He's crazy about you."

"Says who?"

"Says me."

"Then I think you'd better make an appointment with an eye doctor. I'm just someone to help him pass the time until graduation. Once he gets his degree, he'll be heading for the big city and a plum position at some fancy hospital. After that, there'll be plenty of nurses throwing themselves

Sherry Derr Wille

at his feet. For me, I know what my life will be and it won't be anywhere but on this reservation where I belong."

"Now if that's not the biggest bunch of bull I've ever heard. You've fallen in love with him, and you know it as well as I do. Are you going to let him get away from you that easily?"

"Don't tease me, Matt. You know everything I said is true. I have to think about Alex and his future here. If I take him away from the reservation, you know Charlie's dad will cut him off without a cent. I can't have that. You also know on a nurse's salary, I wouldn't ever be able to afford college for him when the time comes. With Ben's backing, he'll at least have a chance in life"

Before Matt could respond, his cell phone rang. Rather than eavesdrop on his conversation, she went out to the kitchen to help her mother make turkey soup with the leftovers from yesterday's dinner.

"What were you and Matt talking about?" her mother said.

"Nothing important. He's worried I'll be an old maid. To be honest I don't know if remaining single sounds so bad."

"What about the young man you told me about when you first got home?"

"I won't deny the fact I think he's special. That isn't the problem. The way I see it, I have a future here and Brand has one somewhere else and it won't include me."

"You know we would never hold you back."

"I know, Mom, but I got my education because of the scholarship from the hospital. When I took it, I promised to come back here to work. I can't and I won't go back on my word. I'm needed here. That's why I've worked so hard to get my education."

* * * *

"Are you sure Jenny's brother is going to meet you here?" Frannie said, as she prepared to head back toward to Madison. "This place looks deserted."

"Of course it does. It's the day after Thanksgiving. Everyone is probably home trying to figure out what to do with all those leftovers from yesterday."

A Father's Love

Frannie laughed at Brand's logic. "Don't remind me of those things. One of Mom's special turkey omelets is more than I can take. It's one of the reasons I wanted to go back to Madison today. Poor Daddy will be eating those things for the better part of the next week. As much as I love Thanksgiving I've always dreaded the leftovers."

Brand knew Frannie made sense. His friends teased about the leftovers their mothers made into weird concoctions, but they could never hold a candle to what his mother did with them. He remembered the turkey and cranberry sandwiches, turkey soup, turkey salad, and turkey omelets, and would never forget casseroles made from turkey, cranberries, and dressing with pasta and cream of mushroom soup. Even their mother had to admit that wasn't one of her better attempts to use up the leftovers from Thanksgiving dinner.

"Well, it looks like you can be on your way," Brand said. "Matt's here. I just hope he found me a relatively cheap motel where I can crash, just in case Jenny's folks get out their scalping knives and make me into leftovers to go with the turkey."

"Oh Brand, don't be so dramatic. Like Mom says, how can they not like you? Besides, it seems like you have her brother on your side." Brand tended to agree.

After Matt parked his car, he got out and waved to Brand and Frannie. "I'm glad you could make it," he said, once he came to where they were standing. "You must be Frannie. Jenny has been talking about you almost nonstop since she got home."

"She's been talking about Frannie, but what about me?" Brand prompted.

"Sorry Buddy, no such luck. Mom and Dad are having enough problems getting used to Karen for her to say anything about you. I'm hoping meeting you in the flesh will make them see how important you are to Jen."

"Does she know I'm coming?"

"You said you wanted it to be a surprise, so I didn't say anything. When I got the call saying you were here, I told everyone that I was going out to meet some of the guys from my high school years."

"Well, big brother, have a great time meeting the parents. I hope you get along better than they did in the movie. I've got a hot young doctor waiting for me in Madison, so I'm planning to get there before dark so we can have supper together at the cafeteria. With luck, there won't be any leftover turkey in sight. I'll see you and Jenny when you get back to the dorm."

Brand watched as his sister got into her car and pulled out of the parking lot. "Were you able to get me a cheap motel room?"

"Didn't look for one. With people coming home for Thanksgiving, most of them are full up, and they often raise the prices for the holidays."

"So if your parents kick me out once they find out I'm white, where do you suggest I spend the next two nights? It's a bit too cold for me to sleep in your car, isn't it?"

"Don't jump to conclusions. Mom and Dad won't kick you out on your butt. Let's see, I'm bunking in with Doug and Alex and Karen is staying with Jenny since Leslie went to spend the holiday with her fiancé, so that leaves the pullout couch. Dad's been all over Mom for buying that monstrosity ever since she got it. The main problem is when she wants to change around the furniture, it takes him and Doug to lift it. The damn thing weighs a ton. He keeps saying since we never have overnight guests to use it, she shouldn't have spent the money for it. Of course, it was one of those times when Mom fell in love with it, and Dad couldn't say no to her. She usually gets her way."

Brand smiled. He could remember a similar argument between his parents when his mother decided she wanted the new furniture for the living room. The pieces she picked out were very heavy, and there had been an ongoing battle over them ever since.

Once he was in Matt's car, Brand began to wonder if this was something he really wanted to do. "If we hurry, we can stop Frannie before she gets to the highway."

"Nonsense," Matt replied. "You drove a lot of miles out of your way to get here. You aren't going to chicken out on me now, are you?"

"Guess not. I just don't want to get Jenny into any trouble over my being here."

"Don't worry. The folks have had a lot to get used to over the past couple of days. What's one more thing to add to the turmoil?"

"What do you mean?"

"Not only did I bring Karen here and announce our engagement, but my cousin is married to Charlie's sister and they told everyone they're going to have Ben's first grandchild. That really hurt Jenny. Of course, it didn't help when Doug dropped the bombshell about choosing Marquette over the UW.

"The old man thinks everyone has to go to the UW, since that's where I went, and where Jenny and Leslie are going. It doesn't matter that we all chose different campuses it still part of the UW system. He seems to think since it's become a family tradition and Doug is being disrespectful in his choice of schools. I think it's great. They've offered him a fantastic scholarship, and I hear their law program is top notch."

"With all that going on, I hope they can find it in their hearts not to turn me out in the cold. I don't want Jenny to know, but I've sent an inquiry to the hospital here, and they seem interested in having me on staff. I'm still sorting out the arrangements, and of course, they could easily change their minds by the time graduation gets here, so I trust you'll keep this just between the two of us. I haven't even told my folks about it yet. I know they'll be happy to have me so close to home."

"Will they? They know, as well as I do, that you could make a hell of a lot more money working in any of the major cities around the state or even in Minneapolis."

"I might make more money, but I wouldn't be close to Jenny. I'm anxious to meet Alex and get to know your family."

"You'd be content to raise another man's child?"

"Why not? What happened between Jenny and the boy's father was over and done with almost as soon as it happened. Anymore there aren't a lot of families where all the kids belong to the same parents."

Matt got a strange expression on his face. From what Jenny told Brand, their mother had been in much the same position as Jenny when she married Tom Red Hawk. He gave Matt not only his name but also his love. If anyone knew about a man raising a son who wasn't his, it was Matt Red Hawk. At least he had something in his favor. Hopefully, Matt could make things easier for him and Jenny.

"At least you've got a good attitude about this. I didn't say a word about you coming, and Jen hasn't said anything about you to Dad. I think she told Mom about you, but she's not the one you have to worry about.

She's talked about Frannie and her studies, but on the subject of a social life and dating, she hasn't said word one. I think she's convinced once the two of you graduate, you'll be out of her life. She's had a lot of disappointments before and has become hard as nails when it comes to guys."

"With Alex's father, I can understand why she's gun shy where men are concerned. I'm different. At least I think I am. We've both been so busy this year, we don't have time for dates much less to talk about the future. I don't know how my sister and my roommate are able to plan a wedding and continue their studies."

Before Matt could add anything more, he pulled up in front of a nice looking white two-story house with Jenny's car parked in the driveway.

"Well, this is it, home sweet home. The house next door is where Jen will be living when she gets out of school. Mom and Dad took care of the old lady who lived there when she was sick. She didn't have any other family around, and when she died, her kids sold it to them for a good price. Since then, they've been renting it out, but the couple who live there are getting a place of their own next spring, and the folks are planning to rent it to Jen when she comes back here after graduation."

Brand looked at the well-kept house and could imagine Jenny living there and taking care of her son. He could also picture himself living there and working at the hospital alongside Jenny. In the past, he'd had aspirations of working in a large city, but once he met Jenny those thoughts went out of his mind. He hoped while he was here, he'd be able to talk to someone at the hospital and see if there was any chance for him to work there as soon as he graduated.

* * * *

Jenny dried the last of the dishes they'd used while making the soup. The bread was in the oven and would soon turn a beautiful golden brown and the fresh bread smell accented the aroma of the soup. She had just hung up her dishtowel when the front door opened.

"Hey Sis, look who I found hanging around the community center."

Jenny came out of the kitchen and stopped short when she saw Brand standing in the living room. "What … what are you doing here?"

A Father's Love

"I rode home with Frannie, and she decided to go back to school. I didn't want to go back and the thought of another of my mother's turkey omelets was more than I could stand. So, I hoped I could bum a ride back to school with you on Monday."

"I ... I guess it would be all right, but where do you plan to stay until Monday?"

"I told him he could stay with us," Matt said. "It would be the perfect opportunity for Mom to try out the sleeper sofa Dad's been having such a fit about her buying."

"Did I hear my name mentioned?" Tom said as he came in the door. He stopped short when he saw Brand. "And just who might this young man be?"

Jenny could sense Brand's uneasiness under her father's scrutiny.

"This is Brand Masterson, my roommate Frannie's, brother," Jenny replied, her nerves making their way into her voice.

Tom held out his hand to Brand. "We're pleased to have to stop in for a visit, son. Will you be able to stay for lunch? If I know my wife and daughter they've been in the kitchen all morning transforming the last of the turkey into some of the best soup you'll ever eat."

"Well, I—"

"I invited Brand to spend the weekend with us," Matt interrupted. "I think it's high time the family meets the young man who is interested in Jenny."

Jenny's heart dropped to the pit of her stomach. With Frannie on her way to Madison, Brand would have no way back to school. From the look on her father's face, she knew Brand wasn't welcome. She instantly began to think of the small motels within driving distance of the reservation and wondered if they would have any openings.

"Well, young man, just what are your intentions toward my daughter? Have you been sleeping with Jenny?"

Brand's embarrassment was evident. Her father's question brought a deep blush to Brand's cheeks, and she knew hers were burning as well.

"Of course we aren't," Jenny protested almost too quickly.

"Mr. Red Hawk," Brand began. "I respect your daughter far too much to do anything like that. I admit I have strong feelings for Jenny, but I would never do anything to go against my own values to say nothing of hers."

"What do we know about your values, young man?" Tom demanded.

"My older sister was foolish and got pregnant when she was still in high school. My mother had just suffered a nervous breakdown and was in no shape to help Suzie raise her son the way you and your wife have been able to help Jenny. She gave him away to a loving couple. It was an open adoption, so Michael knows Suzie is his birth mother, and she gave him to his parents out of love. Jenny was put in a difficult position once, and I would never want to see her in the same situation again."

"Well, you're welcome to stay here. If Matt was the one to extend the invitation, then who am I to put you out? What is your major?"

"This is my last year of residency. Once I graduate in May, I'll be ready to look for a place where I can practice medicine."

Jenny knew her parents had a lot more questions to ask Brand, but she wasn't certain she wanted to hear the answers.

"Is this my daddy?" Alex asked.

His question broke the tension of the moment. "No, Alex, this is Mommy's friend, Brand," she said. "He came up here to spend the weekend so he can meet you. He's heard so much about you, he especially wanted to get to know you."

"Do you like my mommy?" Alex demanded, eyeing Brand suspiciously.

Brand squatted down in front of her son. "I like your mommy a lot. I'd also like to get to know you. It looks like there's some great snow out there. Do you like sledding?"

Jenny watched as Alex's eyes lit up. She knew he liked sledding, because he'd been asking her to take him ever since she got home. She'd planned to go with him after lunch, but she hadn't said anything. The one thing she'd learned as a mother was not to spring things like that on him until they were almost ready to leave to avoid him asking when they were leaving every five minutes.

"I've been asking my mommy to go with me, but she's been too busy helping Grandma. Can we go after we eat lunch?"

Jenny could have cried at how grown up Alex sounded. Maybe school had taught him patience. She certainly hoped so.

"It depends on your mother. If she says it's all right, we can go. If we're lucky, maybe she'll go with us."

Alex looked at her as though praying she would say yes to going sledding.

"I think it's something we can arrange, but you have to eat a good lunch and then find your snow pants. I'll have to find something warm to wear and find something warm for Brand to wear as well."

"Uncle Doug has some warm pants, I know he does."

Jenny smiled to think of how big Doug's pants would be on Brand. It would be easier for Brand to fit into something her father owned, since they had the same slight build.

* * * *

It pleased Brand to see how easily he had won over Jenny's family. Of course, Alex was easy. What little kid could resist going sledding on a sunny winter day? He remembered being a kid and waiting for his father to suggest they go sledding. He certainly couldn't depend on his sisters to want to go with him. Suzie was too boy crazy, and Frannie was too young.

"Come upstairs with me," Matt said. "Between the two of us, I think we can raid Dad's closet and find something suitable to keep us warm. Do you want to join us, Dad?"

"I think I'm getting too old for sledding, but the two of you go ahead. I'm more content to stay inside and feed the fire."

Matt said something about his father getting old and pushed Brand toward the stairs.

"Well, that was easy," Brand said, once they were in one of the upstairs bedrooms.

"Don't get too cocky. The only reason the old man wasn't chomping at the bit to go sledding with us is because he wants to talk to Jenny about you. By the time we get downstairs, he will have convinced Alex that sledding is a guy thing and his mother will only be in the way. It's going to take her some fancy talking to get him to accept the fact she has feelings for a white guy. The only reason Karen passed muster was because of her father's heritage. Now with Leslie, there's no problem, since her fiancé is Sioux from a good family in South Dakota. As a matter of fact, the old man and her fiancé's father have played drums at many of the same pow-wows over the years."

"So I didn't make a hit with your dad?"

"Let me put it this way. It takes a lot to keep Tom Red Hawk away from the sledding hill. I knew he wouldn't be going with us when he got so quiet. Didn't you notice how he quit asking questions? Added to that was his face when you took Jen in your arms and kissed her. I thought the old man was going to have the big one right then and there. Don't get me wrong, he'll get used to you, but don't expect him to bend over backwards for you until he knows you."

"My coming here won't cause any problems between Jenny and your dad, will it?"

Matt laughed at Brand's question. "It would take more than a 'white eyes' to split Dad and Jen apart. He never treated me any differently than any of the other kids, but I always knew Jen was special. She's his first child.

"I'm sure you know he's not my father, at least not my biological father. We've always had a good relationship, even though my real father was a half-breed who didn't think anything of getting Mom in a family way and then leaving her, pretty much like Charlie did Jen. Dad's got to understand this is the new millennium. The kids on the reservation go away to school. Just like Jen and me, most of them will meet someone of a different race.

"Do you think that will happen to Doug?"

"Not my little brother. He's been stuck on Sarah ever since Kindergarten. The two of them getting married is a given. I've done a lot of talking and so have the folks. We've talked them into waiting until they're both done with school."

* * * *

Jen watched as Doug guided Alex out to the kitchen for milk and cookies. She knew it was so Dad could give her the third degree about Brand.

"Why is it we haven't heard you talk about this young man before this?" Tom demanded once Brand and Matt were upstairs and Doug had

Alex occupied in the kitchen. "Is he telling me the truth or are you sleeping with him?"

"One question at a time, please. First, I haven't said anything because I knew you wouldn't approve of me seeing someone of a different race. I hadn't planned to fall for him, but you know what they say about the best-laid plans of mice and men. I didn't say anything because even though I was falling in love with him, I thought he wouldn't be content living here and becoming an instant father. Maybe I was wrong.

"To answer your second question, we haven't been together that way. I spend all my free time studying, and Brand puts in thirty-hour shifts at the hospital. The only time we get together is when he gets a weekend off. Quite often, the only time we get to see each other through the week is when we meet in passing. We live in the same dorm, and my roommate is his sister. Add that to the fact her fiancé is Brand's roommate and we can't very well ignore one another."

"Is it true what he's been trying to tell us? Does he care for you?" her mother inquired.

Jen thought of all the times Brand had professed his love. At the time, she'd been flattered, but she learned the hard way not to put much stock into what men told the women they dated. Through high school, she stayed away from the boys who made fun of the fact she'd given birth to a baby out of wedlock.

By the time she reached college, several male students had asked her out. Each one of them told her they been drawn to her by her exotic beauty. When they wanted to take her to bed, she turned them down flat. It didn't take long for her to be labeled 'The Ice Princess' and 'Miss Cold Fish'. It was no wonder she didn't believe everything Brand told her. How could she know he was, in no way, like any of the other guys she'd dated in the past four years?

"He's been trying to tell me he has feelings for me for several weeks, but I didn't think I dared believe him. I was too afraid of getting hurt."

"Do you think he's serious about working at the hospital here?"

"If it hadn't been for Frannie, I probably would have had doubts, but she said he sent a query letter to the hospital here a couple of weeks ago. I thought she was teasing, I guess she wasn't. Do you think they'll hire him?"

She watched as her father nodded his head. "I was talking to Ben the other day and he said Dr. Weston is retiring, so everyone is being promoted. Ben told me the Board of Directors is worried about where they will find a doctor who would be willing to move up here and accept the low wages they can afford to pay. If I'm not mistaken, I think they will look at Brand very favorably."

"But he's white," her mother protested.

"You know most of the doctors at the hospital are white. Most of the kids who go on to college from our school work hard for their good grades and those grades get them noticed by places away from here. Look at Matt. He worked here for a while until that firm in Appleton noticed him. I don't begrudge him going where he can make the most money. God knows there aren't a lot of opportunities for an architect here."

"So you're in favor of Jenny being with Brand?"

Jen watched her father closely as he considered her mother's latest question. "Graduation next May is six months away. A lot can happen in six months."

Jenny couldn't believe her father's reaction. As long as she and Brand were an item at school, it would be all right. Beyond that, it wasn't acceptable.

"Are you saying you don't mind me being with Brand?" she said, knowing all too well what her father's answer would be.

"He seems like a nice young man," he replied. "I can't say he's someone I would choose for you, but we all know in May you'll be coming back here. It's hard telling where Brand will end up. Face, it, Jenny, you're committed to your people, not to some white man who wants to take you away from your culture."

She nodded. No matter whom she met at school or how she felt, her place was here, among her people. Through their generosity she'd received her education. In no way could she consider turning her back on them.

"You look like you're all ready to go sledding."

Jenny turned at the sound of her father's voice to see Brand, Matt, Doug, and Alex enter the room.

"Brand says we're going to go sledding on the big hill, Mommy, but you can't go."

"Why can't I go?" Jenny said, getting down to her son's level.

"Because it's too dangerous for girls," Alex replied, his voice very serious.

"And it's not too dangerous for little boys?"

"Not with big boys like your brothers and me to protect him," Brand replied.

"Well, I'll have you know I've been sledding that hill since I was a kid and—"

"And nothing, Sis," Matt interrupted, as he put his arm protectively around her shoulders. "This is a 'guy's only' outing. If I'm not mistaken tonight's the 'adult's only' sledding party. You'll get your turn then. In the meantime, we're starved, and the soup and fresh bread smells good. How about fixing us some soup before we hit the hill?"

As much as Jenny wanted to protest being relegated to the kitchen, she held her tongue. Matt knew Brand was coming, and the two of them may have planned this so Brand could meet the family. More important than meeting her family was for him to meet and become acquainted with Alex.

Once they were all seated at the kitchen table, Jenny didn't miss the fact Brand sat in the chair she usually occupied next to Alex. It was obvious Alex wanted his newfound friend to sit there as though it was a seat of honor. Rather than make a fuss, Jenny seated herself across the table beside her mother.

As was their custom, once everyone was seated, her father held out his hands to those on either side of him for the blessing of the meal. She'd never talked about religious beliefs with either Brand or Frannie and was curious to see his reaction. To her surprise and delight, his 'A-men' echoed that of her father.

"This feels like home," Brand said once they started eating. "My father would have expected me to say the blessing to make up for the number of meals I've missed by being at school."

"Do, you believe?" her father said.

"Yes sir, I do. I'm sorry to admit my schedule at school doesn't allow me the luxury of attending services on a regular basis, though. If I'm not working or on call, I'm sleeping."

"What's your specialty?" her mother requested.

Brand swallowed the bread he had just taken a bite of before answering. "Up until a couple of years ago, I was contemplating Pediatrics, but after doing a stint in Family Medicine, I decided I wouldn't be content to treat only children. I could still take care of kids, but I could treat adults as well. There aren't enough doctors out there who enjoy getting their hands dirty with the day to day stuff anymore."

"Have you applied anywhere except here?"

Jenny held her breath. She didn't want to know what Brand was considering. No matter where he went it would be far away from her.

"To be truthful, since meeting Jenny and hearing about the needs of the people here, I've been sending out feelers to your hospital and no others. The feedback has been positive, so I thought this weekend would be a good time to check out the facility and meet the people I've been corresponding with face to face."

Jenny was surprised. Brand's answer actually wasn't anything she'd anticipated.

"I'm afraid you won't make much money working here," her father observed.

"To be truthful, that's not why I went into medicine, and even if it was, one of my student loans comes with the provision that I work for five years in a rural hospital. There's a need for doctors in many areas other than the cities. The idea behind the concept is once the five years are up the doctor will agree to stay. My folks and I discussed it before I applied. They were the ones who helped me make the decision."

Jenny smiled. Brand's answers weren't exactly the ones she knew her father wanted to hear, but they made her happy. That he was considering coming to the hospital where she was committed to serve was something she hadn't heard before. It was one thing for her to have a relationship with a white man in Madison, and quite another to continue it once she returned home. If indeed, he came to work at the hospital here, there was no way they could avoid seeing each other on a daily basis.

With lunch finished, Jenny insisted her mother, as well as Karen, go out shopping for all the day after Thanksgiving bargains, while she tidied the kitchen. As much as she would have liked to go shopping, she needed to be alone to digest the impact of Brand's unexpected arrival and even more his announcement.

A Father's Love

She'd just finished loading the dishwasher and washed the last pan when the phone rang. Out of habit, she answered it, knowing full well no one would be calling for her.

"Hi, Jen," the caller on the other end of the line greeted her. Even though she hadn't heard Charlie's voice in over six years, she recognized it at once.

"Hi, yourself. What are you doing back home?"

"It seems my mother isn't well. I'm sure it was just an excuse to get me back home, but she is my mother?"

"It's too bad you couldn't come for your sister's wedding last summer," Jenny shot back.

"I had to work. Cathy understood, especially when I sent her such a great wedding present. In my business, you snooze, you lose."

Jenny knew all about the wedding present Charlie had sent Cathy for the wedding. It hadn't come until six months after the event, and when it did show up, it looked like something he'd picked up in a thrift shop rather than an expensive gift.

"And just what business are you in?" she finally said.

"Oh, haven't you heard? I'm the top salesman at one of the biggest car dealerships in Chicago."

"So, if you're such a big shot, how did you get away now?"

"Well, you know how the economy is. We all agreed to take a two-week layoff without pay. I'm not like most of those guys I work with. You know how it is, they have wives and families to support. Me, on the other hand, I'm footloose and fancy free."

Jenny held her tongue. She wanted to make a comment about Alex, but she knew better. Outside of her family and a few close friends, no one knew Charlie was Alex's father.

"So, why are you calling me?"

"I thought we could pick up where we left off. You never did give me my going away present. I figured while everyone else is freezing their asses off at the sledding party tonight, we could heat up the sheets. The old man turned that wasted space over the garage into his own private retreat. We could go there and no one would be the wiser."

"Sorry Charlie, I'd rather freeze my ass off. I haven't seen you since the day I told you I was pregnant, and to be truthful, I have no desire to see you now."

"Are you talking about the day you tried to pin your bastard on me? I told you then I wasn't the father. Back in high school, you were a good lay, and I'm certain nothing has changed. I thought I'd give you the opportunity to benefit from everything I've learned over the past seven years. I guess I was wrong."

"I guess you were. Have a nice life, Charlie. Just stay out of mine." That said, she slammed down the receiver, hoping she broke his eardrum in the process.

Chapter Eight

Brand was glad he's practiced his sledding skills with Suzie's kids before Thanksgiving dinner yesterday. At least he hadn't wiped out quite as badly today as he had then.

As soon as he entered the house, he sensed something bad had happened. Jenny's eyes were red and swollen, as though she had been crying for hours, and her mother was consoling her.

"Why are you crying, Mommy?" Alex spoke with the innocence only a child could attain.

Jenny held out her arms to embrace her son. "I was watching a really sad movie."

Brand knew Alex would accept her answer without question, but he didn't. Something had upset Jenny to the point of tears, and sooner or later he would find out just what it was.

Rather than push Jenny in front of her son, Brand went upstairs to change out of his wet clothes. Matt and Doug soon joined him.

"What's up with Jen?" Matt said.

"I asked Mom the same thing," Doug answered. "All she did was shake her head and say that 'little pitchers have big ears'. I figured she meant Alex, so I dropped it right then and there. It must be something serious. You know as well as I do that it takes a lot her cry."

It looked like Matt wasn't ready to drop the subject. "I'll bet it has something to do with Charlie Little Horse. I heard that son of a bitch is back in town."

"Why would he come back now," Doug asked.

71

"I was talking to some of the guys I went to school with, and they said they heard Mrs. Little Horse has cancer and begged him to come home. The funny thing was he couldn't make it back for Cathy's wedding. He told everyone he had to work, but I heard it from a reliable source he was in prison."

Brand inhaled sharply. If this jerk had been in prison, he might be too dangerous to be around Jenny and Alex.

* * * *

"Are you sure you're up to sledding tonight?" Brand said once he had changed out of his wet clothes and Alex reluctantly went upstairs for a nap.

"Don't be silly," Jenny responded. "I'm looking forward to it. Of course, if you don't want to go, we could stay here with the folks."

"No, thanks. I'm all warmed up now. Besides, Matt says the treats afterwards at the community center are worth getting cold again."

"I know what you mean. Mom took a plate of cookies over this afternoon, and Janet Eagle, Alex's kindergarten teacher, makes the very best hot chocolate in the world."

"Hot chocolate?" Brand raised his eyebrows. He wondered if it would be laced with Peppermint Schnapps, the way he and his friends liked to drink it.

Jenny playfully hit him on his arm. "Yes, hot chocolate. This is a reservation remember? We're trying to keep the young guys away from firewater. This party was started when one of the kids went out on the night after Thanksgiving and was killed by a drunk driver. That had to have been at least twenty years ago."

"I remember my folks going. They'd always get a sitter for us kids. They stopped going when Matt was sixteen and old enough to take a date there. Mom said it was so they wouldn't crimp his style, but I figure they thought they were too old for such things. Of course when we don't have enough snow to go sledding, there's a dance at the community center."

"So, why were you in tears when we got home?" From the expression on Jenny's face, he knew his question shocked her. He really didn't care, since he figured the direct approach was the best.

She put her arms around his neck and gave him an unexpected peck on his cheek. "If you promise to drive my car back to Madison, I'll tell you all about it. There's no need to spoil the rest of the weekend with something so trivial."

Brand didn't think something that could prompt Jenny to tears would be trivial, but he let the subject drop. Sunday would be soon enough to find out what had happened.

* * * *

Jenny breathed a sigh of relief when no one else brought up the fact she'd spent the afternoon crying. How dare Charlie call Alex her bastard? He was and would always be their son. If his accusations about Alex weren't bad enough, where did he get the idea she'd be willing to crawl back into his bed? She'd made the mistake of believing his lies when they were dating. Today, she knew better, much better.

She glanced out the kitchen window to see Brand, Doug, Matt, and her father huddled around the gas grill. Her mother had been marinating the venison steaks all afternoon. These were the last of the steaks from the deer her father shot last year and needed to be eaten before the meat from this year's kill arrived from the processor.

Not many years ago, her father would have been grilling the steaks over an open fire in the fire pit. It was during her first year at the University of Wisconsin when her mother insisted they might be Native American, but their heritage didn't mean they couldn't cook like civilized people. Since then, her father became the master of the gas grill. The meat definitely tasted much better since it cooked evenly without burning one side.

Jenny turned back to the salad she was tossing and caught a glimpse of Alex setting the table. The job of setting the table always fell to the youngest in the family. She knew Doug appreciated the fact Alex was now old enough to take over those duties.

"I hope you're all hungry," her father announced as he entered the kitchen with a platter piled high with steaks.

She knew Doug could easily eat two steaks and so could her father and Matt. That left one each for her mother, Karen, and herself and two for Brand. She never saw him eat much, so she wondered if he could even begin to finish them.

As he had at lunch, Alex insisted Brand sit next to him. Jenny was ready to cut up part of her steak for Alex when she saw Brand slice off a chunk of meat and put it on Alex's plate before cutting it into bite-sized pieces.

"I never asked," her father said, once the table blessing was finished. "Do you like venison?"

"I do when it's cooked right. Our neighbors were hunters, and I always looked forward to eating at their house. I remember when they brought over venison steaks for us. Mom tried, but it was terrible. Even Mom admitted she'd rather have Bob and Alice do the cooking when it came to venison."

Jenny's mother nodded her agreement. "Cooking venison is an art. I learned it from my mother and passed it on to my girls. I know I'd be lost if I hadn't been trained by my mother."

Brand looked at Jenny. "Can you fix venison so it tastes as good as this?"

She smiled at the question. "You bet I can, but I have to have a mighty hunter to shoot the deer before I can prepare it."

Everyone with the exception of her father laughed. She knew if she married someone from the area, hunting wouldn't be a problem. If Brand were serious about being with her, would he be able to hunt for the food to fill their table?

"I'll have you know I used to go hunting all the time with Bob and Alice. My dad just wasn't into anything like that. I haven't been hunting in years, but I do know one end of the gun from another."

Jenny smiled. One by one, Brand was breaking down the barriers separating him from her family. She hoped sooner or later he would persuade her father that he cared for her as much as she cared for him.

* * * *

"I called the hospital this afternoon," Brand announced as they walked toward the sledding hill.

Jenny's stomach started doing flip-flops. "I hope this is what you want."

"I do too. I'm meeting with Ben Little Horse and the head of the hospital, Dr. Hawk, tomorrow morning. I'd appreciate it if you'd come along with me. It never hurts to have a friendly face in the crowd."

"I think it can be arranged. I was planning to go over there tomorrow myself. Since I won't be home for Christmas this year, I want to touch base prior to graduation."

"You don't have Christmas off?"

"No, in case you haven't heard, the nurses are no different from the doctors. Thanksgiving was the holiday I drew. I have to work the rest of them just like you."

In truth, she had asked for Thanksgiving as soon as she learned this was the holiday Brand would have off. Of course, she didn't want him to know all her secrets.

At the sledding hill, Jenny introduced Brand to several of her friends. While he positioned their sled for the first run down the hill, she continued to talk to Carol Eagle, Janet's daughter-in-law, until Carol's husband called her name.

Jenny turned back to where Brand stood when someone grabbed her by her arm. When she looked up, it took her a moment to recognize her attacker. Charlie had cut his hair short and tipped it with blonde highlights in an attempt to disguise his Native American heritage.

"Is he the reason you didn't want to go out with me tonight?" Charlie shouted, pointing at Brand.

This close, she could smell the alcohol on Charlie's breath. "I turned you down, because I don't want to go out with you."

"That wasn't the tune you were singing back in high school when you were screwing everything in pants. You wanted to be my girl back then. What's wrong with you now? Are you ashamed to be seen with me because I dropped out of college? Have you turned into a preppy little college girl? Are you a little Miss Goodie Two Shoes now?"

"Look Charlie, I wasn't screwing everything in pants, I was only screwing you. Whatever we had, ended the day I you told you I was pregnant. You didn't want me then. Well, I don't want you now. I told you this afternoon to leave me alone."

She was about to pull away when she felt Charlie loosen his grip on her arm. Before she could react, she felt his closed fist connect with her cheek. The force of his blow sent her reeling backwards. Momentarily dazed, the pain in her face was replaced by one at the back of her head and then complete darkness.

* * * *

Everything happened so quickly, Brand hardly had time to react. One minute Jenny was talking with her friend while he positioned their sled at the top of the hill and the next some lunatic was shouting at her.

Before he reached Jenny's side, the man hit her, and she stumbled backwards. By the time he ran to where she had fallen, Doug tackled the man who hit Jenny. Rather than join the other men egging on the fight, he knelt beside Jenny's prone body.

Portable lights had been installed for tonight's event, and in their glow, he could see blood running from Jenny's nose as well as a red stain in the snow beneath her head.

"Someone call an ambulance," Brand ordered. Several people looked at him as though he'd suddenly lost his mind, "I'm a doctor. We need to get her to the hospital."

Things around him moved in slow motion. From the sounds of the confrontation behind him, Brand could only assume Doug and Matt had things under control with her attacker.

Beside him, Jenny moaned and slowly opened her eyes. "What happened?" Her voice was hardly audible.

"You were assaultcd. When you fell, you hit your head and were knocked unconscious. Now, just lie still until the ambulance gets here. I'm taking you to the hospital to have you checked out."

"What about Charlie?" Her words slurred in a way that concerned him.

As soon as she said the name Charlie, everything fell into place. The man who attacked Jenny was Alex's father. Brand wondered if she would be willing to press charges. He doubted it, but there were enough witnesses he was certain the man would be arrested.

"Don't worry about him now. Just close your eyes. I can hear the ambulance now. We'll have you at the hospital in no time."

It took a lot of talking to persuade the EMTS to allow Brand to ride to the hospital with them, but they relented at last. The deputy who had responded said he'd see Brand at the hospital once Charlie was in custody and transported to the jail.

At the hospital, he was allowed to accompany Jenny into the examination room.

"This is a bunch of nonsense," Jenny protested. "I could have just gone home."

"No you couldn't, Jenny," Dr. Peter Lone Wolf said, as he entered the room. "I just saw your x-rays. You were very lucky you weren't hurt worse than you are, but I want to keep you overnight for observation. From what I can see, you've got a broken cheekbone. I want to x-ray it again in the morning. I hope you won't have anything worse than a black eye and a massive headache. I know you have to go back to school on Sunday, but if someone can drive you, it would be best."

"I'll be doing the driving, Doctor," Brand said before Jenny could answer for herself. "I'm a doctor and will make certain she's checked as regularly as you want her to be once we get to Madison."

"Are you the young doctor who is going to meet with Dr. Hawk and Mr. Little Horse tomorrow?"

Brand nodded.

"Well, I wish you luck. We run pretty shorthanded here most of the time. It will be good to have someone to help shoulder the load."

"Where is she? Where is my daughter?" Tom Red Hawk demanded.

Brand stepped out of the examination cubical to show Tom where Jenny was. "She's right in here, sir."

"I should have killed that little bastard seven years ago when I first learned he got my daughter pregnant and then wouldn't take responsibility for it."

"Calm down, Daddy," Jenny pleaded. "I'm going to be fine. They're going to keep me overnight to make sure I'm all right, and then Sunday, Brand is going to drive me back to Madison."

"Before that, you're going to press charges against the son of a bitch. He'll pay for this. Mark my words, he'll pay."

"Cool it, Dad," Matt said, as he entered the room. "Charlie is in custody, and Jenny is in good hands here. Thank goodness, Brand insisted on calling an ambulance. If Jen had her way, she would have gone back to the house. I just talked to Pete, and he says she's going to be just fine.

She'll have some battle scars, but they'll heal. Let's give Brand and Jen some time alone before we take him home."

Brand watched as Tom and Matt left the room. "They're going to get you settled, so I'm getting kicked out," he said, as he leaned over to kiss her lips. "I wish I would have known that guy was ten miles of bad road. I would have kept him from you."

"Then you'd be here instead of me. Charlie's been mad at me ever since I told him I was carrying Alex. This had been building for a long time. Sooner or later, we were bound to meet. His being drunk didn't make things any better, though I told you firewater wasn't good for my people."

She yawned broadly, and Brand knew the painkiller she'd been given, combined with the sedative was working. With one last good-bye kiss, he grabbed his coat and left the room. He dreaded the ride back to Jen's house. Her father would surely blame him. He already blamed himself.

Chapter Nine

Jenny knew why people hated hospitals so much. Even sedated, she hadn't slept well. This morning, Dr. Hawk ordered more x-rays and again told her she'd been very lucky that the break in her cheekbone hadn't been any worse. Since the eye socket hadn't sunk, there was no need for surgery to repair the damage.

Earlier in the shower, she'd washed her hair as best she could and winced when her fingers touched the now sensitive stitches in the back of her head. She'd been pleased to find the clean clothes her father brought last night to replace her blood soaked ones.

She sat on the bed, waiting for Brand when Mr. Little Horse entered the room. "I'm sorry about what happened to you, Jenny," he said. "If I'd known you were going to be here this weekend, I would have never insisted Charlie come home at this time."

"We would have met again sooner or later."

"I know, and I'm sure things would have been different if Charlie hadn't been drinking. He told me he's changed. I thought it was for the better."

"He hasn't changed, Ben. You know it and so do I. If you're here to keep me from pressing charges, you're wasting your time. Alex doesn't know Charlie is his father. I wouldn't be hurting him. I heard about your wife, but I can't worry about her now. It's my safety that's at stake here. You can't get him out of this one. There were too many witnesses."

"Believe me, Jenny, I wasn't planning to bail him out. There's something you should know. When Cathy got married, Charlie was in prison."

"For what?"

"For beating up his girlfriend. He's been out on probation for the past two months. Unfortunately, this violates his probation, and he'll be sent back to prison to finish the remainder of his sentence. He's looking at eighteen months in addition to whatever he gets for what happened last night."

"I'm sorry, Ben. I really am."

"So am I. I met with the young doctor who came here today. Is he special to you?"

Jenny nodded.

"That's good, because we've offered him a position when he's done with his schooling in May. I hope he's the right man for you and Alex."

"Your wife doesn't know that Alex is her grandson, does she?"

"No, Jenny, she doesn't, and I'd like to keep it that way. It's bad enough for her to know Charlie is going away for a long time. I don't think she could handle knowing Charlie wasn't the good kid she always wanted him to be."

"And now she's dying. I've heard all about her cancer, Ben. It's time for her to know she has a grandson. It almost broke my heart when Cathy told me she was giving you your first grandchild. I gave you a grandchild six years ago, and you can't even admit it to your wife."

Tears formed in Ben's eyes. "Will you be able to come to the house tomorrow? You're right. It's time Mary knows the truth. It's time she knows she has a grandson."

"I'll see. For now, I'm waiting for Brand to come to take me home."

Ben nodded. "I understand. I'll be waiting to hear from you."

Jenny was still shaking from her encounter with Ben when Brand came to pick her up.

"Is something wrong," he asked when he saw how upset she was.

"Not really. Ben Little Horse was just here. He wants us to come to his place tomorrow before we leave and talk to his wife. He thinks it's time to tell her Alex is their grandson."

"How do you feel about that?"

"It's what I've wanted for a long time, but at the same time I'm scared. I've always liked Mary. I don't want to hurt her, but since she's dying, it's best if she knows the truth about Alex. She's already missed so much of his life."

"You said us. Does his invitation include me?"

"It most certainly does. He really likes you. Are you going to tell me you got the job or just leave me hanging?"

"He told you? Oh, honey, we're actually going to be working together here. I know this isn't the time or the place, but I want you to be my wife."

"Your wife? But—"

"There are no buts, Jenny. I love you. I have from the first moment I laid eyes on you. I've talked to everyone I can think of to see how to handle this, and they've all told me if I love you, I have to go for it."

"Everyone?" she said.

"That's right. Let's see, I talked to my sister about the child she gave away for adoption, to my friend Cindy about what it was like to marry outside of her race, and to your brother. The only one I haven't talked to is you, until now. I don't have a ring, but I can get one."

"I think there's still one person to whom you haven't talked."

"Who?"

"My father. I won't let you face him alone. If we're going to be getting married, I think it would be a good idea to have his approval."

"Then your answer is yes?"

Tears flowed down Jenny's cheeks. "The answer is yes, Yes, YES."

* * * *

"You asked my daughter what?" Tom Red Hawk shouted.

"Brand asked me to marry him, Daddy," Jenny replied before Brand could say anything.

"I know how you feel about Jenny marrying outside her race," Brand said, trying to keep his voice calm. "I love her and have since the first time I saw her. I've planned my life to be close to her and have accepted a position at the hospital here on the reservation for after I graduate."

"Listen to him, Dad," Matt intervened. "I knew he loved Jen the first time I saw the two of them together. It takes a special kind of a man to fall in love with a woman who has a child. For what it's worth, Doug and I both like him, and you saw how Alex reacted to him. I think Brand is exactly the man Jen needs in her life."

"But he's not of our people."

81

"Charlie is of our people and what has he done for me? First, he denies his son, and then he hits me. Brand loves me, and even though I've tried to deny it, I love him. I know I'm committed here, but I think Brand has shown he's also committed to our people."

Brand watched as Tom's shoulders slumped in defeat.

"I'm going to be twenty-two soon, Daddy. I don't need your consent, but I would like your blessing."

"Would you get married without your mother and me present?"

"You know I wouldn't. It's not as if we're going to marry before either of us graduate. With our schedules at school, neither of us would have time to be newlyweds. Brand works thirty hour shifts and between being on the floor and in the classroom, I have no time to socialize, to say nothing of making a home for a new husband."

"Don't be too hard on your folks, Honey," Brand said, putting his arm around her shoulders. "I can understand where they're coming from. It's hard for parents to accept their child is involved with someone so different. Not too long ago I attended the wedding of my friend Cindy. She married a boy by the name of David Chi. I thought open hostilities were going to erupt at the wedding. His grandparents came to San Francisco directly from China, and no one in the family was thrilled with David's pick for a wife. Believe me, they came to love her, and she and David couldn't be happier. We have to give your folks time to adjust to the fact that we're in love."

"So was this why you came here?" Jenny's mother said.

Brand was beginning to feel like he was on the witness stand and being cross-examined by the best trial lawyer in the state. "No it wasn't. I came here to meet you as well as Alex. I admit I applied at your hospital in order to be close to Jenny. I figured once we were working together, I could make her understand how much I care for her.

"Last night when I saw that jerk hit her, the thought of losing her made me sick. Thank goodness the damage was minor, but it was enough for me to realize I wanted to protect her for the rest of our lives."

Jenny's father nodded. "I can understand what you're saying. I'm sure you know Matt isn't my son. I felt the same way about Betsy when I first met her. It didn't matter to me knowing Matt came from another man. What mattered was I had fallen in love with her. You kids have six months

82

until graduation. Once graduation is behind you, we can talk about a wedding. Let's get Matt and Karen married first."

Brad breathed a sigh of relief. At least telling Jenny's parents hadn't resulted in blows. He'd expected acceptance to be a lot harder.

"Since you've told us," Betsy said, "don't you think you should give your parents a call, Brand?"

"I guess we should. I think they had an idea of what was going on when I was home."

He pulled his cell phone out of his pocket and placed the call to his folks. He told them. When Betsy indicated she wanted to talk with his mother, he passed her the phone.

"Mrs. Masterson," she began, "I'm Betsy Red Hawk. Since your son has asked our daughter to be his wife, I think it would be best if we all met. The kids will be going back to school tomorrow afternoon. Do you think we could meet for an early dinner in Wausau?"

Brand watched as Betsy listened to what his mother was saying.

"Yes," she finally said, "we know George's Restaurant. We could meet there at four tomorrow afternoon...We're looking forward to meeting you, as well."

She handed the phone back to Brand.

"Jenny's mother sounds nice," his mother greeted him. "It will be good to see you again. As a matter of fact, it works out really well, since your sister wanted to drive over to Wausau to have dinner with us before they leave. You know their favorite place to stop is George's Restaurant. We'll see you then."

Brand groaned. It would be bad enough for his parents and Jen's parents to meet, but the thought of Suzie and her family being there was doubly bad. Oh well, they would all have to meet sooner or later.

"I almost forgot, Ben Little Horse asked us to come over and see them tomorrow," Jenny commented. "Maybe I should call over there and see if we can come right after church rather than in the afternoon."

Jenny had hardly spoken the words when the doorbell rang. Brand was surprised to see Mr. Little Horse standing in the doorway with a woman who could only be his wife.

"Oh, Jenny," Mary Little Horse said as she entered the room and went immediately to Jenny's side to embrace her. "I'm so glad this is all out in the open. I've always suspected Alex was my grandson. It's a relief to know the truth. I have a lot of lost time to make up for with Alex."

"I tried to tell her you two were coming over tomorrow, but she didn't want to wait that long," Ben said, after shaking hands with both Tom and Brand.

It was hard for Brand to imagine anyone as nice as Ben and Mary could have a son who was as much of a jerk as Charlie.

"There's something I think you should know," Jenny said. "Brand came here not only to interview at the hospital, but also to get to know my family and especially Alex. He asked me to marry him today, and I said yes."

Brand watched the expression on Mrs. Little Horse's face. "From what Ben tells me, this is one exceptional young man. I just hope he's up to the challenge of being white in a Chippewa world."

"I think I am, Mrs. Little Horse."

"Please, call me Mary. I want to get know you better, and I think I will be seeing a lot of you, both of you."

"What do you mean?" Jenny said.

"There's nothing more anyone can be do for me here. We went to Florida to think about what we should do. When we got back, I applied for and was accepted into an experimental program for cancer research at the University Hospital in Madison. I figure if I have to go down there, I should have some friends to visit me when they aren't working. Besides, I did some checking, and you're next rotation is on the oncology ward. I think it would be rather nice to have my own private nurse."

Brand assessed the woman who stood before them. It was evident her cancer had progressed to the stage where experimental medicine would be her only hope. Last year he did his round in oncology and decided it wasn't for him. Cancer was an enemy and one he didn't have the stamina to fight. He prayed the doctors at the UW would be able to help Mary. She was a strong woman.

"What about Charlie?" Matt said.

"Charlie is a fool," Ben replied. "I looked the other way when he got Jenny pregnant. I should have insisted he marry her, but instead I sent him away to school and secretly helped my grandson however I could. I can't look the other way this time. It's true, he spent time in Waupun and I kept it a secret, but those days are over. He's on probation, and he'll be going back to serve out the remainder of his sentence. The corrections office has been contacted, and they will be here on Monday to take him back to prison. For now, we have no son, only a fine grandson who will make us proud."

"Don't talk that way, Ben," Mary pleaded. "Before we came here, I went to see Charlie at the jail. He wants to see you before he has to go back to prison, Jenny."

The expression on Jenny's face told Brand the last person she wanted to see was Charlie, but at the same time, she didn't want to disappoint Mary.

"I'll go with you," Matt offered before Brand had a chance to say anything.

Jenny looked up at Mary. "I hope you understand, but I don't think I want to see him. He made his feelings perfectly clear last night at the sledding hill. He doesn't want anything to do with either our son or me."

"He was drunk last night," Matt said. "I'm sure he sees things differently by the light of day."

"He most certainly does," Ben interrupted. "He's feeling sorry for himself and wants Jenny to tell him she won't press charges against him. I was with Mary at the jail, and I listened to what my son didn't say. Charlie is worried about the same thing he's always worried about, his own sorry hide."

"I don't agree," Brand finally said. "I think you should see him. Let him see what he did to you, and tell him you won't let it drop."

Jenny looked as though the idea of facing Charlie, even though he was incarcerated, frightened her. "Of course you're right. Will you come with me?"

"You know I will. I won't let you face your worst nightmare alone."

Chapter Ten

After church on Sunday, Jenny, Matt, and Brand went to the jail so she could see Charlie. Although she had been apprehensive about such a meeting, it relieved her to be ushered into a room where she would sit on one side of a thick glass with Charlie on the other side.

Jenny gasped when he entered the cubical, wearing an orange jumpsuit. She certainly wasn't prepared to see him dressed the way she'd seen prisoners on the news, yet she shouldn't have been. He was a criminal and as such wasn't allowed to wear street clothes. Once seated, Charlie picked up the phone mounted on the wall and motioned for her to do the same with the matching phone beside her.

"Are you happy?" he said as soon as he picked up the phone. "This is all your fault, you know."

"What do you mean it's my fault?" she shot back, trying to keep her voice calm.

"If you hadn't been there with that 'white eyes,' I wouldn't have lost my temper. Why did you bring him here?"

"Look, Charlie, who I'm with is my choice. At least I'm not trying to hide my heritage, and I don't talk like I'm in a bad 1950's cowboy and Indian movie. You're an educated man, not some kid, trying to sound like Tonto."

"Why are you with a white man? Do you think you're better than me because I dropped out of college and you're going to graduate in May?"

"I never said any such thing, and like I said before, it's my choice."

"Maybe you didn't say it, but you're thinking it. What about the brat?"

A Father's Love

"If you're talking about 'our' son, his name is Alex. He knows nothing about you, but thanks to all of this, he will get to know his paternal grandparents. Your father has been more than generous, but he hasn't been a presence in Alex's life. Last night he finally told your mother the truth. Now Alex will have two sets of loving grandparents, to say nothing of a mother and father."

"Father? What man on this reservation will want you when they know what a whore you are? I said it when you first told me you were pregnant and I'll say it now. With the snap of my fingers, I can find any number of guys to say they slept with you and they're the father of your kid."

"You're a bigger fool than I thought you were. In case you haven't heard, there's DNA testing, although I don't have to have anything like that done to know you're Alex's father. You're the only man I've ever been with, at least until now. I'm engaged to be married and—"

"And you'd let a white man raise your child?"

"He'd be a hell of a lot better father than you are, Charlie. At least he has a job and hasn't been to prison for God only knows what. I came here as a favor to your mother. I can see I should have gone with my first thoughts and stayed away from you. I expect you to stay away from me and my son in the future."

Without making further eye contact, Jenny replaced the phone and broke the connection with Charlie. More than anything else, she wanted to be out of this room and away from the monster her first love had become.

"Are you all right, Sis?" Matt asked when she turned away from the window.

Jenny couldn't think of anything to say. Charlie had called her a whore and again disowned his son. Of course, she wasn't all right. Instead of saying anything, she merely nodded her head and allowed Brand to take her in his arms.

"What did that bastard say to you?" Matt pressed.

"It doesn't matter. He's where he can't hurt me. I just want to get out of here."

Instead of turning toward the door, Matt picked up the phone. "What did you say to my sister?" he shouted into the receiver.

She turned back in time to see pure hatred radiate from Charlie's eyes.

"Nothing my ass. It had to be something or else she wouldn't be so upset."

Matt was silent for a several long moments, before he again began to speak. "You're lucky you're behind this glass, and I can't get to you. If it were up to me, I'd knock some sense into that thick head of yours. Thank God my nephew will never have to acknowledge you're his father." The slamming down of the receiver rang throughout the room.

"What…" Jenny started, but the looks on both Matt and Charlie's face told her he related their conversation almost verbatim to her brother. "How could he tell you terrible things like that?" she demanded.

Matt took Jenny's arm. "It doesn't matter. Nothing matters except you and Brand getting back to Madison and forgetting any of this ever happened."

Once they were out of the visitation room, it was Brand who asked what Charlie had said to both Matt and Jenny.

"It was just like things were when I told him about Alex. He called me a whore and said he would get his friends to admit I'd been with them sexually. It's over now. After what's happened here, I doubt he'll ever come back to this area. He'll be going back to prison, and this is the last we'll hear from him."

Matt voiced his opinion to the contrary, loud and long, but Jenny refused to believe him. Charlie's parents would more than likely disown him, and he'd be a fool to come back again.

* * * *

Brand was concerned about Jenny. After the confrontation with Charlie at the jail, he worried today wasn't the day she should meet his parents. The problem was he couldn't ask the questions burning on his mind with Alex buckled securely in the booster seat behind them.

Instead of saying anything, Brand thought about his proposal of marriage to Jenny. It certainly wasn't the kind of proposal he'd imagined. He planned to come here and meet her parents, get the job, and get to know Alex. Once he got back to Madison, he was going to ask his parents to send him the antique engagement ring he inherited from his grandmother so he could ask Jenny to marry him at Christmas.

A Father's Love

The proposal came too quickly, without any romance behind it whatsoever. After seeing what Charlie did to Jenny, he knew he had to be the one to protect her as well as Alex. He no longer wanted to wait until Christmas to ask her to be his wife.

By jumping the gun, he waited to place another call to his mother until everyone went to bed leaving him alone in the living room. Once he did, he asked her to retrieve the ring from the top drawer of his dresser and bring it with them today. Since Jenny agreed to be his wife, she deserved to wear a ring on the third finger of her left hand.

"I think Alex fell asleep," Jenny said, breaking into his thoughts.

He glanced over his shoulder to see the child sleeping peacefully before he said anything. "Are you sure about this? We could contact both sets of parents and call this thing off until you're less upset."

"That's nonsense. I've been dealing with Charlie's attitude and refusal to acknowledge Alex for the past six years. What he said today is no different from the accusations he made when I told him I was pregnant. I'm just glad he'll be somewhere far away from my son and me. Thank goodness Alex will have a father figure in his life who can teach him the way a man is supposed to act."

Brand smiled at her response. It was pleasing to think she considered him worthy of being a father figure in her son's life. "I want to give him a good life. With us working together at the hospital and your mother living right next door to help us out with Alex, we'll do just fine."

"Do you really want to live next door to my parents? You haven't seen the house, but it's very small. Big enough for two but I doubt it will be right for a family of three. We'll probably be tripping over one another."

"Of course, I do. It's an excellent starter house. Your dad asked the people living there if I could see it after he calmed down about my asking you to be my wife. When we went through, we saw a few things I told him I'd like to change. He said he'd help me with the remodeling. He also offered to pay for it, but I told him if we intended to make the place our home, it was only fitting that I pay for what I wanted done."

Jenny giggled. "And just what do you want done?"

"For starters, you have to admit the kitchen is rather outdated and the bedrooms are really small. The back yard is large enough we can put on an addition and still have enough room for Alex to play with his friends. Your dad agreed with what I was thinking. He said he had some friends who were in the construction business and thought he could get us a good price on the work."

Brand could tell from the expression on her face she was already imagining the changes he wanted to make in the house. Were they something she considered asking her father about having done? He hoped so. After seeing the house and voicing his opinions about the renovations, he envisioned her working in the kitchen and raising their children, including Alex, in the larger bedrooms he planned on adding.

They continued to talk about the future and when they would be ready to start planning a wedding until they finally reached the restaurant. The caravan of cars that followed them down from Lac du Flambeau included her parents and Doug, as well as Matt and Karen.

Once they parked, he saw his parents and Suzie and her family pull in and park next to them.

"How's that for timing?" his father said as soon as he got out of the car.

"I can't believe we both got here at the same time," Brand replied.

Once everyone else got out of the cars, Brand made the necessary introductions. He breathed a sigh of relief when Tom was the first to hold out his hand in greeting.

"Your son has asked my daughter to marry him," Tom said. "I can't say he's the man I would have chosen for her. I don't like her marrying someone who isn't of our people, but Brand seems to be sincere. As my wife said, I can't interfere if this is the man Jenny wants in her life."

"I know what you mean," Brand's father responded. "I wasn't happy with the man my oldest daughter married, but Ron turned out to be a standup guy after all."

Ron stepped up and shook hands with Tom as well as Doug and Matt. Brand knew his brother-in-law tolerated the teasing he got from the family.

"I'm certain Jenny is going to be a more welcome addition to this family than I was, but I've overcome the obstacles. I know Brand, and after talking to him on Thanksgiving, his feelings for Jenny are true. We didn't think he'd ever find a woman who lived up to his high standards, but Frannie assured everyone Jenny is definitely the woman he's been looking for."

While the men continued to talk, Brand's mother gave him a hug in greeting. Once she did, she slipped the box with the antique ring in it into his coat pocket.

"Thanks, Mom," he whispered in her ear.

* * * *

Jenny wondered if her family had been as overwhelming to Brand as his was to her. His mother, Anita, reminded her of Frannie, while his father Christopher was an older version of Brand.

"I'm Brand's sister, Suzie," the woman who was only a little older than herself said before embracing her.

"I would have known you anywhere. You look so much like Frannie it's uncanny. Brand told me about your situation. It's one of the reasons I was able to accept his love. I worried about him accepting Alex." She glanced toward the back seat of her car where Alex was starting to wake.

Jenny tried to go to her son, only to see her mother heading toward the car. It broke her heart to think Alex was more comfortable with his grandmother than with her. Maybe he would have been better off if she had given him up for adoption right after he was born.

The counselor at the school had suggested just that, but her parents were adamant about her raising the boy. She prayed once her schooling was finished, she would be a true mother to her son.

"He's used to being with his grandmother, isn't he?" Anita said.

"With me at school, Mom has been his surrogate mother, but after graduation everything will change. In the meantime, he e-mails me every day. Unfortunately, it's not the same as being together on a daily basis."

Anita's gaze shifted from Alex to the bruise on Jenny's face. "Are you certain you're feeling well enough to join us for dinner?" She put her hand tentatively to the bruise.

Jenny smiled. "It's not as bad as it looks. My cheekbone is broken, thus the bruising. There's nothing the doctors could do about it. I just have to get used to the pain and wait for the bruising and swelling to go away. The pain pills help. I'm so glad Brand is doing the driving, since I shouldn't drive while I'm taking them."

"I'm so sorry this happened to you, dear. Of course, if it made my Brand realize he cares for you, something good came out of it."

Anita's comment was confusing to Jenny. "What do you mean?"

"Christopher and I would have to be deaf and blind not to know our son has fallen in love with you. He was burned once, and we were afraid he would throw himself into his work like he has with his studies and forget love is as important as a career."

Before Jenny could question Brand's mother about that, she felt Alex tugging on her pant leg. The look on his face was filled with questions. She knew he wasn't used to seeing strangers. There were rarely visitors to her parents' home who were unknown to him.

Jenny squatted at her son's side. "This is Brand's mother and the man with Grandpa and Brand is his father."

The look in Alex's eyes turned from questioning to awe. "He has a Mommy and Daddy just like you do. I don't have a Daddy, but I would like one."

"I know you would," Jenny replied, trying hard not to cry.

What had she done to her son? It's not like he was any different from the rest of the kids in his class, but it still wasn't right.

"Do you think Brand would be my daddy," Alex continued, oblivious to the thoughts running rampant in her overactive mind. "I really like him, and he likes me too."

"Did I hear my name mentioned?" Brand said, as he joined them.

Alex nodded. "I asked Mommy if you're gonna be my daddy. I don't have one, but I'd like it if you were my daddy."

Jenny's heart ached. Her son deserved a father and Brand certainly fit the bill. If she'd brought home other boyfriends over the years, would Alex have so easily bonded with them?

"I was hoping you'd approve of me, Alex," Brand said, squatting next to Jenny to be at Alex's level. "I asked your mommy to marry me. She said yes, but before I give her a ring, I want your permission."

Alex threw his arms around Brand's neck and hugged him tightly. "Can we still live next door to Grandma and Grandpa? Will I still get my own room? Will I still be Chippewa?"

Brand returned Alex's hug, then got to his feet. Once upright, he lifted Alex off his feet and held him with his left arm. "You bet you can help.

A Father's Love

We'll talk to your grandpa about it right after we have something to eat. As for not being Chippewa, nothing can ever take that from you. It's one of the reasons I love your mother so much. Nothing will ever change your heritage. It's what makes you special, and don't ever forget it."

Still holding Alex, Brand looked lovingly at Jenny. "I know you said you'd marry me and since Alex is in agreement, let's make it official."

With his free hand, he reached into his pocket and produced a blue velvet box. From the look of it, Jenny knew it was old. The covering had a sheen that said many people had handled it over the years.

"Don't open it now," he said, once the box rested in her hands. "I think you need to sit down, doctor's orders. You look tired, and I don't want the excitement to be too much for you."

Everyone agreed with Brand and moved into the restaurant to continued getting to know one another. Once they were seated at the table, Brand tapped his glass for attention.

"Outside, I gave Jenny a gift, but I didn't want her to open it until we were all together."

Jenny fingered the soft exterior of the box. Once she opened it, she knew her future would be sealed. Her hands shook. Trying to ignore the trembling, she flipped open the lid to reveal the treasure hidden inside. With it opened, she gasped at the beauty of the ring nestled inside.

"Oh Brand, it's beautiful. It's just that it's too much. It's..."

"It's what my grandmother wanted. This ring has been passed down through our family for generations. The story is my great-great grandmother got this ring on her fifteenth birthday from my great-great grandfather before they left England to come to the United States to settle."

"But what about your mother?"

"Christopher's parents were still alive when we got married. His mother wanted me to have it, but I insisted it belonged on her finger as long as she was still married. That's when she promised to give it to her first-born grandson. I've kept it for Brand ever since her death fifteen years ago."

"Then I accept it. I don't feel worthy of anything so beautiful, but I'll wear it with pride."

Jenny watched as Brand took the ring that had to be at least two carats from the box and slip it onto the third finger of her left hand. The antique setting was a mixture of gold and silver filigree, and the stone sparkled as though it had just come from the jewelry shop.

She had no doubts that Anita took it to the jeweler to have it cleaned and checked in anticipation of Brand needing it to seal their engagement.

Around the table, everyone seemed to be talking at once, and her family all took turns looking at the ring Brand put on her finger. When, at last, the waitress came to take their order, Brand took the opportunity to take her in his arms and seal their now official engagement with a kiss. It was a promise of a bright tomorrow for the two of them as well as for Alex and any children they might someday have.

* * * *

Brand relaxed once the dinner with the parents finally came to an end, and they were on the road heading back toward Madison. Only days earlier he'd worried about meeting Jenny's family, and within the span of two days, she met his. Luckily, both families accepted them, although he thought her father would have been happier if there were some trace of Native American blood in his background.

"Your mother made an interesting comment while your dad was talking to my dad," Jenny said.

"Comment?"

"She said you'd been burned by love in the past, and she was afraid you were never going to fall in love. Do you want to tell me about it? I mean, you met the skeleton in my closet. Do I have the right to ask about yours?"

Brand took a deep breath. He wondered when Claudia would raise her ugly head again. "You have the right to ask about anything. We're going to be married, I don't intend for us to have any secrets between us."

Jenny let of a sigh of relief. "It doesn't matter, really it doesn't. I was just wondering is all."

"No, you deserve to know everything about me. I was planning to tell you. Mom moved up the timetable a bit. I was in my senior year in college when I met Claudia. I thought she was the love of my life, but I was mistaken. She was a freshman and knew my folks had a lot of money. At first, she pressured me to have sex with her, but I declined. I knew what happened to Suzie, and I didn't want to be known as the man who had gotten Claudia pregnant. She kept insisting if I loved her, I'd make love to her, but I was determined to stick to my guns. Instead, I went home, got the ring, and took it back to school with me. I told her the only way I'd make love to her was if we were married, and I proposed. When I held out the jewelry box, she refused to take it. She said if she couldn't have a ring she picked out in a real store, I didn't love her enough. I knew right then and there I'd made a horrible mistake. I wanted to have sex with her so badly I mistook lust for love. I vowed then and there not to let my body rule my mind again."

"And now?"

"I won't tell you any lies, I do want to make love to you, but not until we're married. In the past, I haven't even dated anyone. That is until I met you. I've fallen madly in love with you as well as with Alex. I want us to be a family. The sex part can wait until marriage. I'm not one of those guys who thinks he has to try out the merchandise before he buys it. That kind of crap is for kids in junior or senior high school. We're adults, and we can wait until we're married to play house."

"Oh Brand, those were exactly the words I wanted to hear. We both have ghosts in our past lives. I have Charlie and you have Claudia. Now that we've put them to rest, we can move on with the rest of our lives. I do love you, Brand. More than you'll ever know, and no matter what, we're going to make this work."

Chapter Eleven

Although Jenny wore the beautiful ring Brand gave her on the third finger of her left hand, she didn't have time to bask in the afterglow of their engagement. Her studies, as well as time on the floor, consumed all her spare time, and Brand continued to work thirty-hour shifts at the hospital. When they did see each other, they were too tired even to consider planning a wedding.

In January, Mary Little Horse came to the hospital for the experimental therapy. During her stay, Jenny visited often and shared stories about Alex. Unfortunately, they both knew the treatments were too little too late and by March, Mary went back to the reservation to spend her final days at home.

The weekend of Easter, Jenny didn't have to work and went home to attend Mary's funeral. It was a bittersweet ending to what began at Thanksgiving. Back then, Mary accepted Alex as her grandson. Unfortunately, Alex hardly got to know his paternal grandmother before she passed onto the next life.

Now at long last, May arrived, and Jenny could begin her real life. It was no longer one filled with studies and hours on the floor at UW Hospital, but a life that included being a mother to her son.

"Today is your graduation day," Brand said when he appeared at her dorm room door.

Jenny rushed to his outstretched arms. "Don't you have to work?"

"I managed to switch schedules with someone so I could be there. I have another week and then I'm done as well. I talked to Ben Little Horse, and he told me they're expecting me at the hospital the second week in June. I'm planning a quick trip out to San Francisco to see my friends Cindy and David before I report to work."

Jenny knew about his plans to go to California. They'd talked about it and agreed it would be good for him to take a trip and relax before starting work. For the first time, all of their plans seemed real. The only problem she could foresee was where he would stay. They weren't married, so living together would be completely out of the question.

"Where will you be staying once you get back from California?"

"Ben said I could get a room with him until we're married and our house is ready to move into."

"You'd stay there?"

"I will until I can find an apartment close to the hospital. You have to admit, I haven't had much time for apartment hunting with my schedule."

"Another thing you haven't had time for," Frannie said, "is planning your wedding. You know Mom and Dad are looking forward to hearing the two of you say 'I do'."

Jenny smiled. Next weekend Greg and Frannie would be getting married and moving to Superior where Greg would be working in the clinic, while Frannie would be a Pediatric nurse at the hospital.

The Monday after Frannie and Greg's wedding, Jenny would be starting work as well. For the first time in any of their lives, they would be adults, making their own way in the world and beginning their new lives.

* * * *

Brand sat in the audience with his parents and Greg, while Jenny's family sat three rows away. One by one, the new nurses walked across the stage as their names were called, and they received the degree that would allow them to put the initials RN behind their names.

Sitting there, he recalled the conversation he'd had with his sister this morning. Both he and Jenny had been so busy finishing their degrees that they hadn't had time to think about wedding plans. He didn't know how Greg and Frannie had managed planning a wedding, to say nothing of finding a place to live in Superior.

If a wedding wasn't so important to both sets of parents, Brand was tempted to book a flight to Las Vegas and take Jenny there on their first weekend off to tie the knot.

"What are you thinking, Little Brother?" Suzie said, leaning over to whisper in his ear.

"Where do you want me to start?"

"How about your future with Jenny?"

"I was thinking about what things are going to be like once we get married and how we're going to plan a wedding while we're both starting our new careers?"

"You'd better have a talk with Mom. She and Mrs. Red Hawk have been talking on the phone just about every day. I think they're planning to spring it on you after the ceremony. She did remember to tell you they have a joint graduation party planned at one of the restaurants here in town, didn't she?"

"Of course she did. Why do you think I moved heaven and hell to get this entire weekend off? After next Friday, I'll be a full-fledged doctor, and I can leave the dorm and UW behind me."

"Then the real work begins, or so I've been told. Do you think you're ready to start working at the hospital on the reservation after you get back from seeing Cindy and David?"

"What's that supposed to mean? You know I'm ready. This is what I want and working as a doctor on the reservation will keep me closer to Jenny. That's where our future lies."

"Are you sure you're not going to miss the big money you could be making somewhere else?"

"Look, Sis, I didn't get into medicine for the money. There's a need there, and I think I can fill it."

"That's all I wanted to hear. You'll be really happy about the plans Mom and Mrs. Red Hawk have been making."

As much as Brand wanted to question Suzie further, his mother's loud Ssh cut their conversation short. While he tried to concentrate on the new nurses crossing the stage, he couldn't help thinking about what would be announced at the party both sets of parents had planned for Jenny and Frannie.

A Father's Love

"Miss Francis Masterson," the Dean of Nursing announced just prior to Frannie crossing the stage to the beginning of her life as a nurse.

Greg and Brand were immediately on their feet cheering with the rest of the family. Frannie's day had come and soon Jenny's name would be called. The future for both of them was bright, not only in the field of nursing but as wives and mothers, once they were united in marriage to Greg and Brand.

* * * *

"We have an announcement to make," Jenny's mother said, once everyone toasted both Jenny and Frannie. "We know you children haven't had a lot of time to think about a wedding, so Anita and I have been making some preliminary plans, all subject to your approval, of course."

Jenny gasped. How could her mother and Brand's mother take over the planning of her wedding? Instead of saying anything, she decided to hear her mother out. How many plans could they have made without input from either herself or Brand?

"Well," Anita began, "we thought a fall wedding would be perfect. That would give you both time to get settled into your new jobs. It would also give Brand and Tom the opportunity to get the remodeling done on the house."

Jenny almost choked on the sandwich she was eating. Their parents had taken on the job of planning not only the wedding but also the remodeling of the house. She and Brand hadn't even had time to discuss what their plans for the future were.

"What do the two of you think?" Betsy said.

"We really don't know what to think," Brand replied. "The wedding is something we need to plan, but school has kept us too busy to think about it. As for the remodeling, I was talking to Matt about it on the phone. Between the two of us, we've come up with a plan I think will work."

"What about me?" Jenny protested. "I haven't seen these plans. Don't I get a say in this?"

"Of course you do," Matt said. "If you open your present, you'll see what we've been working on."

Jenny's fingers trembled as she opened the package from Matt and Karen. In it, she found a scale model of the house next door to her parents. The difference was that it was much larger than the house she remembered from her childhood.

"This is the prototype and beneath it are the blueprints for the changes we'll have to make," Matt explained. "Brand told me what he was thinking about and I put it on paper. We both know nothing will even be started until you give the thumbs up on our plans."

Jenny looked everything over. The house was exactly what she wanted in a home. The rooms had been transformed from small and cramped to spacious and inviting. There were four large bedrooms and a truly modern kitchen, along with a family room, complete with a working fireplace.

"This is beautiful."

"It's also going to be a lot of work," Brand added. "If our mothers are hoping for a fall wedding, we'll have to work fast. You and Alex can't move in until it's finished."

"Then what are we waiting for?" Jenny said. "I love the design. The sooner we get started the sooner we can get married and move in together."

Chapter Twelve

Jenny stood at the back of the church with the other bridesmaids in Frannie's wedding. Each of them wore a pastel dress of a different color making them look more like a spring bouquet than young ladies who were about to walk down the aisle for a wedding.

Frannie's friends from high school were willowy blondes with fair complexions and blue eyes. She alone stood in direct contrast with her darker skin, brown eyes, and blue/black hair. It pleased her that Frannie insisted she wear pastel yellow, while the other girls wore pink, lavender, blue, and lime green, with Suzie wearing peach.

Being the first one to walk down the aisle, she could tell her appearance was shocking to the people in attendance. She and Matt stood in direct contrast to the rest of the wedding party.

Although she'd met Brand's parents and his older sister, there were grandparents, aunts, uncles, and cousins who would be shocked to learn he was going to marry someone of a different race.

Ahead of her, at the end of the aisle, Matt stood waiting for her. His reassuring smile gave her the confidence to keep walking without turning tail to run out of the church before the questioning glances turned to statements she wasn't ready to hear.

At the end of the line of groomsmen, Brand smiled and winked at her. She knew he loved her as much as she loved him, but how would he feel once his family made comments he wasn't prepared to hear.

Once the remainder of the bridesmaids, as well as the matron of honor, came to the front of the church, the entire congregation rose as Frannie started the walk to her future. Her smile was radiant, and she glowed beneath the sheer veil. The gown she wore was an off the shoulder dress with an overlay of lace and a train stretching halfway down the aisle of the church.

Jenny had been in the weddings of her friends before, but there had always been so much excitement, she hadn't listened to the words of the vows the couple said. Today, she was more observant. She and Brand would be saying these words to each other within a matter of months.

The words, 'in sickness and in health', had an impact on her because of their chosen professions, but not the same as the ones 'for richer or poorer'. If Brand hadn't met her, he would have been much richer, because he wouldn't have even considered a position on the reservation. Doctors in large cities made good money, while those who worked among the poor didn't make much more than their patients.

It was true the poverty level wasn't as low as it had been when she'd been a child. Ben Little Horse changed the lives of the people on the reservation by providing good paying jobs for his employees. Of course, the casinos also provided jobs for her people, but still the hospital didn't always have the funds to pay their employees an income comparable to their counterparts in the private sector.

"I now pronounce you man and wife. You may kiss your bride," the minister said before asking Gregg and Frannie to face the congregation. "It is my pleasure to be the first to introduce Gregg and Frannie Thomas."

Jenny smiled when the guests burst into applause.

After Greg and Frannie started back down the aisle as husband and wife, everything moved at what seemed like warp speed. It took only moments for her to move toward the center of the aisle and take Matt's arm to make her own walk to the back of the church.

"Did you take notes?" Matt said.

"I listened carefully. How about you? Your day will be coming up next month."

"Of course I did. It's a big step we're taking this year."

Jenny didn't have time to reply because they were now standing in front of Greg and Frannie to wish them well. Jenny wasn't at all upset about not having to endure the reception line. The bridal couple acted as ushers, greeting each guest as they left their pews. Jenny had seen it done only once before and thought it made a lot more sense than making the entire wedding party stand and greet people they didn't know.

"You look beautiful," Brand whispered, as he put his arm around her waist and kissed the back of her neck.

"You don't look so bad yourself. I think we should invest in a lot of peach colored shirts for you to wear to the hospital."

Brand wrinkled his nose. She knew he didn't like the color shirt he was wearing with his tux, but like every other man in the wedding party, he hadn't had much choice.

"I don't think so. I'm not really into peach, but yellow is certainly your color."

Jenny only smiled, since a woman who looked a lot like Brand's mother was bearing down on them with a vengeance.

"You certainly made a lovely contrast in the wedding party, dear," the woman said taking Jenny's hand between hers. "From what I hear, we'll be coming to another wedding this fall."

"Jen, this is my Aunt Pearl," Brand said, making an attempt at an introduction.

"I'm pleased to meet you," Jenny replied, shaking the woman's hand.

Pearl reached over to take Jenny's left hand in her own. "I'd forgotten how beautiful this ring is. I told my sister it was a shame Brand hadn't found a woman to love enough to give it to. I'm so glad the two of you are going to be married. You have to know I've been worried about my nephew. I was beginning to think he was one of those men who like other men more than women."

"You've nothing to worry about, Aunt Pearl. I'm not gay. I'm just picky. It wouldn't have been fair to get married while I was in school with nothing to offer a woman, other than a husband who spend long hours at the hospital and expects her to support him. As it is, Jen and I will both be working at the same hospital."

Pearl beamed at that and moved on. The confrontation wasn't nearly as bad as Jenny expected. If the remainder of Brand's family were so accepting of her, the reception would be rather enjoyable.

The next person in line could have been a clone of the rest of the bridesmaids. Her blond hair and slender figure stood out in direct contrast to the man behind her. He was definitely Oriental. His complexion was more golden than white, and his eyes had a slant to them.

"I'm Frannie and Brand's friend, Cindy Chi, and this is my husband, David. You have to be Jenny. Brand has told me so much about you I feel like we're old friends. Has your family accepted him yet?"

Jenny was caught off guard. "My dad was ready to have a coronary, but when Brand played Sir Galahad and saved me from a former boyfriend, all was forgiven. It really helped when he went out to help Dad fix steaks on the grill and admitted to liking venison. Of course, my brother, Matt, met him in Madison and helped pave the way with the folks."

"I'm sure we'll have time to talk more at the reception, but believe me, what you and Brand have will make you a great couple.

* * * *

Brand relaxed. He'd been worried about how his extended family would react to Jenny, and now he was pleasantly surprised. In their many phone conversations, David and Cindy asked him all the same questions he'd been asking himself about his decision to marry outside of his race. Having them play devil's advocate had given him a lot to think about. In the end, they both gave him their seal of approval to his choice of a life partner. He looked forward to spending some time with them after the wedding when he went out to California to visit.

After the last of the pictures were taken, they finally arrived at the reception. He wished he was sitting next to Jenny, but being the best man for this affair kept him far away from the bridesmaids who were sitting at the other end of the table.

He decided there were definitely perks in sitting at the head table, because they were served first. Rather than the usual ham sandwiches served at affairs like this, the prime rib melted in his mouth. He knew his parents hadn't been exactly excited about the choice of menu, but Greg's parents had been the ones to pay for this extravaganza.

With dinner ended, Brand was finally able to make it to Jenny's side. "I've missed you," he whispered in her ear once they were on the dance floor.

"I haven't been too far away," she purred back.

"I know, but any distance is too far. I honestly don't want to wait until October, to be with you on a full time basis, but I know planning a wedding takes time. Do we really have to go this fancy?"

Jenny giggled at his question. "I doubt it. I was thinking something a little more along the lines of a traditional Chippewa wedding."

"I'm almost afraid to ask what that entails."

"You should be. Mom said she's been going through the attic to find the wedding clothes she and my dad wore for their wedding. They were the same ones her mother and father wore. The dress is white doeskin with beading matching the beading on the shirt you'll be wearing. Of course if you're not comfortable about it, we can go with the tuxedos and long dresses."

"I think it sounds perfect. When I was a kid playing cowboys and Indians, I always wanted to be the Indian. My friends always laughed at me. Guess I'm getting the last laugh after all."

They danced for several more numbers before Brand felt someone tap him on his shoulder. "Are you going to keep this lovely lady all to yourself or can I have a dance with her?"

Brand looked up to see his best friend since childhood, Colin Rogers, standing beside him. "You know I don't like to share, but as long as you remember I saw her first and she's mine, I don't see the harm."

Colin held his hands up in mock surrender. "When have I ever moved in on your territory? I just want to have the chance to dance with the most beautiful woman here."

Brand backed away and watched Colin take Jenny in his arms. He didn't want to appear too possessive, but he didn't like the idea of Jenny being with anyone but him. After the fiasco with Charlie at Thanksgiving, he'd become even more protective than he had ever been of anyone in the past.

"You look like a lovesick calf," Cindy said, as she pulled him out onto the dance floor.

"I guess I am. After Jenny's run in with the ex-boyfriend I'm really paranoid about any other man being with her."

"I think she's safe enough with Colin. You did know he came out of the closet last year."

Brand nodded. He remembered all too well the shock of finding out his best friend was gay and had been living with a guy for the past three years. If gay marriage were legal in Wisconsin, Brand was certain he would be attending another wedding this summer.

He glanced across the room to where Colin's partner, Anthony, was involved in conversation with another of their friends from high school. Just being at home with the people who had been in his circle in high school, brought not only memories of the past but also thoughts of what they had all become.

He and Cindy had found love outside their race. Colin was involved in a lifestyle that was alien to everything they'd been taught in their quiet middle class white homes. Added to that, Billy Moore had been killed in action in Iraq, and Jeff Anniston was serving in Afghanistan. The kids from his group of friends had all grown in different directions and were leading lives far from what their parents envisioned when they were all hanging around together.

Chapter Thirteen

Being home was exactly what Jenny needed. Although her work started right away, she didn't care. It took her mind off Brand's trip to California and the fact he wouldn't arrive until two weeks after she did.

Once he returned, the work on their new home began in earnest. Her father and his friends helped Brand with the remodeling of the house. It didn't matter how late the crew worked, her son was always there, 'helping' with whatever work the men were doing on his new home.

"Are you sure Alex isn't being a pest?" Jenny said to Brand as they shared their lunch in the cafeteria.

"Positive, he's really a lot of help. Besides, he gets a real kick out of bringing us the sandwiches your mom makes. Do you think she'll be sending us care packages once we're married?"

"Don't you think I can cook?"

"I don't know. You're really busy at the hospital and won't have much time for cooking."

"Well, some of the food Alex brings over is stuff I prepared, so get ready to be spoiled when we're finally married."

"Is this a private party or can anyone join it," Dr. Karl Hawk asked as he approached the table.

"Nothing private, Karl," Brand replied.

"Good, I wouldn't want to interfere. I thought maybe you were in a deep discussion about wedding plans."

Jenny laughed at his comment. "Unfortunately, the wedding plans are very low on our list of priorities right now. We're up to our eyeballs in the remodel of the house we'll be renting from my parents."

"I'd heard about that. I was wondering if you could use a spare pair of hands."

"We aren't turning away any help we can get," Brand replied.

"Good, because my son is home from college and bored out of his mind. When we remodeled our house last summer, he was invaluable."

"He sounds like a gift from the gods, but we can't afford to pay him."

Karl laughed. "Hell, I'll pay him to get him out of the house. He saw the work being done on the house you're working on and asked me to find out who was doing it. He wants to volunteer to help. In high school, he worked for a construction company doing some work on the new condo complex in Woodruff. He knows what he's doing and really wants to help."

Jenny reached across the table to put her hand over Karl's. "We never turn down willing help," she said. "We can't pay, but the food is worth working for."

"I'd worked for the food. I've eaten your mother's cooking at some of the potluck suppers we've had at the church. Don't be surprised if my wife and I stop over when we have time."

They finished eating their lunch while talking about the plans they had for the house and discussing them with Karl. Jenny wondered how they got so lucky.

She knew his son, Michael, and remembered when he was working for the construction company. As she recalled, Mike was a good kid and would be a great help. She wished they could afford to pay him, but knowing Mike, he wouldn't take the money if they offered it.

* * * *

By the time Jenny got home from the hospital, Mike had joined the crew working on the house.

"Hey Jen, thanks for letting me come over and lend a hand," Mike called from atop the ladder.

"I was surprised when your dad offered your help. You should have known you'd be welcome here."

"I wasn't sure if you were using professionals, and if you were, I didn't want to step on anyone's toes." He came down from the ladder and gave her a hug. "Alex is a great kid. He's a lot of help, too."

"What are you buttering me up for?"

"Maybe a second piece of your mom's apple pie. She brought it out for lunch, and it was really good and…"

"And since you're a growing boy I think I could persuade her to bring out an extra slice with supper that is if you're staying for supper."

"Of course I am. I've only been here since eleven this morning. Besides, my dad wants me to meet your fiancé."

"Brand? Why?"

"Dad's pushing me to become a doctor, and he thinks Brand will be a good influence on me. If the truth were known, I'm already planning to get into a premed program this next year. I just don't want to puff up his ego too much. How much longer do you have before the wedding and you need to have this project finished?"

"To be honest, Brand has been staying here at night and burning the midnight oil working on this place. We're planning the wedding for the second Saturday in October. That gives us about two months. Do you think we can get everything done by then?"

"Maybe not everything, but enough to make you comfortable. I've got most of this month left so I can put in a lot of hours. It takes my mind off the amount of work I have ahead of me once I get back to school. We'll get it done. You've got a good crew working here."

Jenny thanked Mike and headed for the house to change into work clothes. At the door, she almost collided with Alex.

"Whoa, where are you headed in such a hurry?" She scooped her son up into her arms.

"I have to get back to help with the house. Grandpa says I'm the most important worker. He called me a gopher, and he says it's one of the most helpful things I can do for him."

Jenny smiled. She knew her father called him a go for, meaning he was sent to bring things the men working on the house needed, but if Alex thought he was a scurrying little animal, it did no harm to allow him to continue the fantasy.

Alex wriggled free from her grip and headed back out to where the men were working.

"I was surprised to see Mike Hawk come over this morning," her mother greeted Jenny.

"Me too, but Karl asked us about it at lunch, and we couldn't say no. Come to think of it, Mike said he'd been here since eleven. We didn't talk to his dad until after twelve."

Her mother laughed. "You tend to forget Mike played football with your brother in high school. They're good friends. It's possible they ran into each other at one of the parties going on around town."

"If that's the case, I'm sure Doug would have told Mike he was welcome anytime. Maybe his dad was just being polite in asking Brand and me first. Whatever, I'm certain we can use the help."

Her mother agreed and returned to fixing homemade pizzas for supper. Since Brand insisted in buying all the supplies for the remodel as well as providing the food to feed the work crew, her mother didn't mind doing the cooking. At the same time, her father refused to take any money from Brand for the rent even though he depended on the rent money to pay the monthly mortgage. Even so, Jenny tried to slip her mother money every payday to help with Alex. They'd decided to keep it their secret because her father would have been upset to know she was paying money in addition to what Brand spent on the remodel.

* * * *

Brand changed from the scrubs he preferred to wear in the emergency room to a pair of jeans and a polo shirt. He was just leaving the doctor's lounge when he ran into Karl.

"My wife and I were wondering if you could use another two pair of hands tonight."

"We can always use the help, Dr. Hawk, but we couldn't impose on you."

"I don't know why not, but only if you call me either Hawk or Karl when we're off duty. I only asked you about having Mike come over so I could see what you'd been doing over there. I'm a bit like my son. I'm like an old fire horse. All they have to do is yell fire, and I'm ready to get into the action. Since we finished the remodel on our place last year, I've been itching to get my hands wrapped around a hammer. My wife, Lori, is the same way about decorating. She's looking forward to talking to Jenny about what kind of furnishings you're planning for your place, as well as what colors she has in mind for the rooms. She's got an eye for such things."

"When you put it that way, how can we say no? From what I heard this morning, Betsy is making homemade pizza for supper. If I know her, she's got enough to feed the fifth division."

"Sounds good to me. I'll give Lori a call and have her meet us there."

Brand headed for the parking lot to give Hawk some privacy for his phone call. As he did, he shook his head. The longer he lived on the reservation, the more the people here amazed him.

Just when he decided he knew everyone working on the house, he came home to a whole new crew. Sometimes there would be men from Tom's place of employment, other times he'd find kids who went to school with Doug. Everyone was ready to lend a hand, even if they only worked a few hours at a time. At this rate, the house would be ready for them to move in as soon as they were married.

He thought of the long nights he'd spent alone in the house. When he had said he'd be getting an apartment, Tom suggested he stay at the house during the construction. It wasn't an ideal situation, but at least he wasn't paying for an apartment on top of the cost of the remodeling. He knew he'd be glad when he and Jenny were married and the bedroom would be furnished with more than a lumpy hand-me-down mattress and a sleeping bag.

The drive from the hospital to the house was a short one, but it gave him time to wind down before digging into the real work of the day. At the hospital, his challenges were mental, while here they included manual labor.

At the house, he saw Doug and another young man who had to be Mike Hawk. They were busy up on ladders putting the roof on the new addition.

"Hey, Brand," Doug called as Brand got out of the car. "We've got some experienced help. I'll bet we can get this done in no time flat."

"Don't be too sure of that. To get ahead of schedule, you'll have to work day and night for the next month, and I intend to get some sleep along the way. I can't sleep with you pounding on that roof."

"Welcome home," Jenny said as she came out of the house next door.

"Thanks. I think you'd better set another couple of places at the table. I just found out we've got two more volunteers coming tonight, and I said they should come for supper."

"Who in the world are you talking about? I thought everyone on the reservation has been here at one time or another the last couple of weeks. To be truthful, I think they've come only to get some of Mom's good cooking, but who am I to turn anyone away?"

"It's Hawk and his wife, Lori. He asked me if they'd be welcome and I told them yes."

Jenny's surprised expression made her look much younger than she actually was. "Well, they're the last people I expected to be coming over. Of course, I heard they did a great job on remodeling their home last year. I was going to talk to Lori about what she thought about the best way to decorate this place."

With Brand off to help the guys with the work, Jenny went into the house to tell her mother about the extras coming for supper.

"Oh dear, this certainly isn't fancy enough for Hawk and Lori. I went to their place when they held their open house to christen the remodeling. Everything was so perfect, I felt really out of place."

"Come off it, Mom. Hawk and Lori know we're in a mess here. They're coming to help, not take high tea."

Leslie looked up from spreading the sauce over the pizza dough. "Jen's right, Mom. Nobody expects a construction zone to be fancy. I went their open house too, you know. It was meant to impress, but I was in the same class as their daughter, and they're just down to earth people. I can hardly wait to see what Lori has to say about the decorating of Jen's new house."

Within ten minutes, Hawk and Lori arrived. As Leslie and Jenny both said, they were dressed to work, rather than for a fancy dinner.

"When Hawk called and said that we were welcome, I pulled some monkey bread dough out of the freezer. I thought it would go well for dessert. I'm so excited you two kids are going to be living so close to your folks. What are you doing for furniture? I know you didn't have much at school."

A Father's Love

"Tom got me new living room furniture," Betsy began, "so I'm giving the kids my old stuff. It's still in pretty good shape, and it will get them started."

"Oh, that's great. I know of a shop in Woodruff where they have great used stuff. We got a lot of our furnishings there when we remodeled. I didn't want new because it just doesn't have enough character. Besides, used is affordable and well made. I saw a dining room set over there the other day. It needs refinishing but that's minor. The price was right. I told them to hold it until I could talk to you about it."

Jenny was shocked to realize Lori did something so wonderful for her. Over the years, her mother refinished several pieces and Jenny helped. She enjoyed it and could hardly wait to go to the shop Lori mentioned.

Chapter Fourteen

By the time Doug, Leslie, and Mike had to return to school, the majority of the remodeling was finished. The only thing left to do was to paint and move in the furniture.

While her parents were on their cruise, Jenny and Leslie refinished not only the dining room set Lori had found at the used furniture store, but also the furniture for the master bedroom and for Alex's room as well.

"It's beginning to look like a home," Brand observed, when they finished painting Alex's bedroom.

Jenny looked around the bare room now waiting for the furniture to arrive. Bright red and bright blue walls with huge flatheads of Spiderman on one wall and Cars on the other provided the themes Alex wanted. She told Brand the cost of such things was far too much, but he insisted. Since Alex couldn't make up his mind, Brand wanted him to have his two favorites in his new room.

"It will feel more like a home when we start moving in the furniture. We only have two more rooms to paint, and we'll be ready to go. I dread moving those old appliances back into the kitchen. Everything looks so new and perfect, I'm afraid they won't fit."

Brand smiled. "I've been keeping this a secret, but I guess now is a good time to tell you. My folks want to give us new appliances for our wedding present. Dad said since he couldn't help with the hands on remodeling, like your folks have, he wanted to do this for us. They're coming up this weekend to take us shopping. I hope you know what you want in there."

"You're kidding. I can't believe they would spend so much money."

"What you don't understand is my parents are loaded. They spend big on their kids. Frannie got the down payment for a house, when they find one they want, for her wedding present. You'll get used to my folks. They've worked hard for their money and are more than willing to share the wealth with their kids. I gave up protesting about the amount they spent on gifts a long time ago."

"You're right. It will take a lot to get used to that. With my folks, there was never enough money to buy all the things they wanted. The cruise they took this summer was something they saved for, just like their new furniture."

"So, do you know what you want? When we did the kitchen design, we allowed for a side by side refrigerator, as well as a dishwasher."

"I like the looks of the new stainless steel appliances. I just can't believe we're going to have everything I've ever dreamed about."

"Speaking of dreams, don't you think you should let me in on some of the plans for our wedding?"

Jenny smiled. She'd been planning the perfect Chippewa wedding, at least perfect in her mind. She loved the Community Presbyterian Church where she had grown up learning the Bible not only in Sunday school but also during the services.

"Mom and I have been scrounging through the attic for the wedding clothes she and my father wore. Would you be comfortable wearing traditional Chippewa clothing?"

She watched Brand's expression as he considered his answer. Ever since they found the wedding clothes, she had envisioned him as a beautiful blonde Indian dressed in the fashion of her people. Over the past weeks, she called Frannie as well as Leslie and asked them to be in the wedding. Leslie already had regalia she could wear, and Frannie said they would be coming next weekend to see if there was something in Jenny's wardrobe suitable for her.

"I think it sounds perfect, but what about Greg? He is my best man, you know."

"I have that covered. I got a call from Frannie this morning, and they're coming up this weekend so she can go through my closet for a perfect dress to wear. When I knew they were coming I called Matt so he could help Greg find something."

"You were pretty sure I'd go for this, weren't you?" Brand said, as he took her in his arms.

Jenny smiled. "I was hoping you'd go for it. If not, I planned a traditional wedding as well. I saw a dress I really wanted when I was shopping with Lori in Woodruff. If you said no, I planned to go shopping with Leslie and Frannie when they got here. Since you agree with my plans, it will save us a lot of money."

"That's what I love about you," Brand said before kissing her.

His kiss left her breathless and wishing the wedding wasn't over six weeks away. If they were already married, they could go to their bedroom and make delightful love.

"What do you love about me?" she probed.

"Let's see, you're practical, you like to save money, you know how to make our wedding something special. How much more do you want from me?"

Without waiting for her answer, he kissed her again, leaving her even more wanting of sexual satisfaction than she'd been before. The wedding couldn't come soon enough to suit her.

* * * *

Brand worried about his parents, the pillars of Pinehurst society, coming to the reservation. They knew where he had decided to work, but were they ready for their son to be in the minority. He doubted it. They'd met Jenny's parents and became instant friends, but how would they feel once they realized their son was one of the few whites in this community?

Knowing his mother's passion for casino gambling, he reserved a room for them at the Lake of the Torches for the weekend. Greg said he'd bring a sleeping bag and bunk at the house while Frannie would be staying with Jenny.

He saw the last patient for the day and was leaving the clinic when he ran into Karl Hawk.

"I hear you have the entire weekend without being on call," Karl greeted him.

"You heard right. My folks are coming to get us our wedding present, and my sister and her husband are coming up to help us make plans for the wedding."

A Father's Love

"Lori told me about Jenny's plans. How do you feel about dressing in traditional Chippewa clothing?"

"If you asked me the same question a year ago, I would have said no way, but being here has made me change my mind. This is the heritage of the woman I love and the patients I see in my office every day. I can't imagine practicing in any other environment."

"I was hoping your answer would be something like this. I've known Jenny since she was a little girl. In my book, she deserves the best. To be honest I was hoping she would find someone of her own heritage, but after what Charlie Little Horse did to her, I'm pleased she's found someone like you to love."

"I take that as a high compliment. My family will be here for the weekend. I'd like it if you and Lori could join us for a cookout at Tom and Betsy's place Saturday night. I think my parents would like to meet you."

"I'll check with Lori and have her get in touch with Betsy about what she can bring. Thanks for the invitation. Something tells me you have family to meet, and if I don't get home to take Lori out for a fish fry, my name will be mud. Just wait until you're married and you'll see what I mean."

By the time Brand reached home, his parents' car sat in the driveway next door. As usual, Jenny parked in the driveway of the house they would share once they were married, so he knew Pinehurst society had already meshed with Tom and Betsy's Chippewa culture.

Before going next door, he stopped at the house long enough to take a quick shower and change into more comfortable jeans and a tee shirt.

"Are you sure you're off for the entire weekend," Jenny asked when Brand entered the house.

"Positive," he replied, taking her in his arms. "The only way I'll get called in is if we have a complete disaster. Now, I'm starving. Is everyone ready to go out to eat?"

"You bet we are," Frannie said as she came out to greet him. "Do you know how hard it was for both Greg and me to get the weekend off to come down here to see you? I'm planning on you feeding me and feeding me well."

"I don't think there's a problem there. I made reservations for the Back Bay Cove at six. Karl told me they have a great fish fry on Friday night."

"I know you planned to be the host for this party, son, but after seeing how you've been spending your money, I think it's best if your mother and I pay for dinner tonight," Chris, Brand's father said. "Tom took me on a tour of the house. I can honestly say it wasn't what we were expecting. You mother was afraid you'd be living in a tee-pee. I have to admit I had no idea what to expect. It's going to be quite the house once you're finished. I wish you would have let your mother and me help you with the expense, but I know how independent you've always been. Of course, we'll make up for that tomorrow when we go to the furniture store."

"Your father's right," his mother added. "I've seen the pieces you already have and I think your house will be beautiful. I can't believe Betsy wants to get rid of such a beautiful living room set, especially the couch."

Everyone from Jenny's side of the family laughed at that.

"If you knew how many fights that couch has prompted, you wouldn't wonder," Betsy said. "I wanted it so badly, and when we got it home we realized it needed Tom and both of the boys to move it. I almost feel guilty for pawning it off on the kids, but they've assured me they really want it, especially since it's a sofa sleeper. It will be a while before they will be able to afford to furnish the two extra bedrooms, so this seemed like the perfect solution. Something tells me they expect to have some overnight visitors."

"Since you're getting rid of this furniture, what are you going to do for a living room set?"

"Don't worry about Betsy," Tom interjected. "She's chomping at the bit for the kids to get married because she has new furniture just waiting to be delivered. Of course, once the painting is done in the living room over there, we can move this stuff out of our house and into theirs. That's when the work begins here. Before we have anything delivered Betsy wants the room painted and the carpeting replaced. I never knew buying new furniture would open such a can of worms."

The discussion of furniture continued as they all piled into their cars for the drive to the restaurant. Frannie and Greg rode with Jenny and Brand.

"I know your folks came up here this weekend to talk about kitchen appliances, but I think they're getting hung up on the furniture we've inherited from my parents," Jenny said. "How do you think they'll react when we tell them we're planning a service with not only a minister but also a shaman and we're going to wear traditional Chippewa clothing?"

"Dad will suck it up and ask if you can find something for him. Mom is more traditional. She'll be upset for a few minutes until she sees some of the beautiful outfits you've been sending me in pictures. Which one did your sister think would be best for us?"

Jenny described the dress Leslie had chosen. She hoped it would meet with Frannie's approval as well. Since her friend, Linda Fox was going to make the clothes for the wedding party, Frannie and Greg would have to go there for a fitting.

"I can't believe it's the same one Greg and I liked so well. I was really worried about the color of the beading in the other one you sent a picture of. This will be perfect."

"I like the idea of not having to dress up in a monkey suit," Greg said. "I wore one at our wedding, but it doesn't mean it was comfortable. I can hardly wait to wear your traditional garb. It will make for a unique wedding."

* * * *

Dinner was a great success and soon the discussion of furniture was set aside and in its place was one about clothes for the wedding.

"Betsy tells me you're planning a traditional Chippewa wedding," Brand's mother, Anita, said as they were finishing the last of the fish and fries.

Jenny's stomach started to do flip-flops. From what Brand told her about his parents she knew they were far from her own family both in their standing in their relative communities and their financial status. How would her future mother-in-law feel about them having a wedding that was the furthest thing from Frannie's formal wedding as they could possibly get.

"It's what we've been talking about. I've always wanted to be a traditional Chippewa bride and Brand is humoring me

"Well, I think it's great. Your mother and I have been discussing the dresses we'll wear, and she promised to take me to the seamstress before we leave so I can pick out something. I have to admit, it will be different, but I've never denied my children anything they've ever wanted. With Frannie, it was a big wedding with all the trimmings. With Brand it will be a traditional Chippewa wedding. If nothing else, we can't be accused of doing things the same as everyone else. This wedding will be the talk of my friends for years to come."

"Is that good or bad?" Jenny was still not quite clear about her future mother-in-law's position on their wedding.

"It's a good thing," Chris assured her. "If nothing else, I know my wife well enough to know she enjoys doing things other people will find unconventional. This wedding of yours will be her crowning glory."

Jenny relaxed. Their wedding would be the way she wanted it, and even though Brand's family were high society, they weren't turned off by the idea of doing things in the traditional Chippewa way.

* * * *

On Saturday morning, Brand and Jenny rose early and drove out to the casino to pick up his parents. Tom assured them he and Betsy would meet them at the appliance store in Woodruff since they were going into town to arrange for the delivery of their new furniture as soon as their present living room set they was moved over to Brand and Jenny's house.

Brand knew Jenny was apprehensive about meeting his parents for appliance shopping, but he kept assuring her they only wanted to get what Jenny wanted because she would be the one using them.

The selection the store offered was impressive. After much deliberation, they finally agreed on the stainless steel finish for the stove, refrigerator, and dishwasher. Brand could tell Betsy was jealous of the dishwasher. Their house wasn't equipped with one.

"So," Tom said, "I suppose you want one of these, too."

"It would be nice, but we can always have the holidays at Jenny and Brand's place and use theirs."

Everyone laughed at that, but by the time they left, Tom had purchased a dishwasher for his wife and was making plans to remodel one of the cupboards in the kitchen to accommodate it.

"Are you sure about this," Jenny asked, once the appliance order was written. "All of this costs a lot of money. We could have gotten along with something less expensive."

"Don't worry about it, honey," Brand said. "This is something Mom and Dad want to do, and believe me, they can afford it. Besides, your folks have done so much by helping with the remodeling and giving us the living room furniture. It's only fair. Just remember this is our wedding present."

Brand hoped he put Jenny's mind at ease. He accepted the fact his parents came off as extravagant, but he knew for Jenny wasn't accustomed to such lavish spending.

"I tend to agree with Jenny," Betsy said. "These appliances are very expensive."

"Expensive, yes," Anita replied, "but they'll last a lot longer than getting something inexpensive. When we were first married and pinching pennies, I remember buying the cheapest appliances we could get. After five years, two burners on the stove quit working and the refrigerator's compressor died. That's when we finally listened to Chris' father and invested in something designed to stand the test of time. Since we can afford to do this, there's no need for the two of you to learn the same lesson."

"Anita makes sense," Tom said. "When we were first married, we didn't have enough money to buy quality appliances. As I recall, your mother and I made do with used and replaced them more often than we wanted. I can see what Chris and Anita mean. They can afford to give you the best, and it's what should be done. You'll be happier in the long run with things you don't have to worry about having to replace anytime in the near future."

Chapter Fifteen

Jenny woke and realized this would be the last morning she would spend in her parent's home. By three this afternoon, she and Brand would be husband and wife, and their life would revolve around the house next door. She would be the one cooking the meals and keeping the house clean.

Across the room, Leslie still slept peacefully. Not wanting to wake her sister, Jenny slipped out of bed and tiptoed into the hall. From the window, she looked down on the backyard. The tree with Alex's swing stood in the same place with its leaves chased by the wind, falling in a golden shower swirling around the yard.

After today, everything would be different. From downstairs, she smelled coffee brewing and bacon frying. Without thinking, she stopped at Alex's room to see if he was still asleep. She smiled as she remembered, Brand had insisted Alex spend the night at the hotel with the rest of the men. For today, she would be a single woman without a child to consider. Tomorrow, Alex would again be with her parents, and she and Brand would be spending their one-day honeymoon in Minneapolis. She hurried down the stairs and made her way to the kitchen.

"I didn't think you'd be up this early," her mother greeted her.

"I didn't either, but I guess I'm just too excited to sleep. I can't believe by this time tomorrow I'll be a married woman."

"I suppose I should be giving you the mother daughter talk, but considering you have Alex in your life, you're like I was when I married your father and had a son of my own. With things the way they are in the modern world, the daughters know more about what goes on in the marriage bed than their mothers do."

"It does seem like a shame to think the innocence of our children has been corrupted. Of course, I'm sure in the past other cultures insisted the woman be pregnant before marriage in order to assure she was fertile. I think it was meant more to assure the tribe of its future existence. It's a bit barbaric, but the way things are today, it seems like we've gone back to the same line of thought. I am so lucky you and Dad insisted I get my diploma and my degree rather than forcing me to marry Charlie. I see so many of my friends who tried the marriage route or didn't have supportive parents and are now living hand to mouth and depending on food stamps to get along."

"I know what you mean. It's hard for the young girls who get into trouble if their parents don't step up to do the right thing. So many of them end up in really abusive relationships or are shunned by the very people who should love them. Are you and Brand planning on expanding your family?"

Jenny thought for a moment before answering. "We'd like some time to get to know one another as husband and wife, but we understand the need for Alex to have a brother or sister. We aren't going to try to prevent pregnancy, at least not until we have a child of our own. We think it's important for Alex to be a big brother rather than an only child."

"It sounds like you have things well planned. For now, let me pamper you for one more day. What would you like for your last breakfast as a single woman?"

Jenny looked at the counter where her mother was mixing pancake batter. The question was completely unnecessary. She loved her mother's homemade pancakes. Of course, there were the frozen pancakes she heated up in her microwave, but they couldn't compare to the recipe her mother used ever since Jenny was a little girl. Her mother gave her several recipes, including the one for pancakes, which she tucked behind their respective headings in the box Matt had made for the recipe shower her friends gave her. As a new bride, she knew she wanted to make the homemade meals she ate as she grew up, including her mother's pancakes.

As she savored the fluffy treat, Jenny wished Alex were here rather than at the hotel with Brand and the rest of the men from the wedding party. She knew how much he enjoyed his grandma's pannycakes, as he called them.

"A penny for your thoughts," her father said as he entered the room.

"Oh, they're worth a lot more than a penny, Dad. I was thinking this will be the last meal I have in Mom's kitchen as a single woman. In a few hours I'll be married and running my own home."

"You know you and Brand are always welcome to come home for a meal. I'm afraid your mother is going to have a hard time adjusting to making meals for the two of us instead of a house full of you kids as well as Alex."

"I know, Dad, but I'm a big girl now. I'm going to enjoy playing house for real and being a mom to Alex as well as a wife to Brand."

* * * *

The beauty of the church was almost overwhelming when Brand and the rest of the men from the wedding party arrived an hour and a half prior to the service. Pumpkins, corn shocks, and colorful mums were everywhere. In the corner was a ceremonial drum, along with the piano as well as the flutes he knew would be played as part of the ceremony.

He'd planned to have Alex as his best man, but was told he needed someone who could be a witness and, as a child, Alex couldn't sign the papers. Plans were changed to make Alex a miniature groomsman, while Greg acted as the best man. Matt was the other groomsman and Doug, along with Ron, acted as the ushers.

On Jenny's side of the aisle, her sister, Leslie, would be the maid of honor, while his sister, Frannie acted as bridesmaid. His sister, Suzie, on the other hand was Jenny's personal attendant. The wedding was a complete family affair.

He'd been shocked at his mother's acceptance of the non-traditional wedding he and Jenny had planned. Being the cream of Pinehurst society, he'd expected open opposition. Instead, she agreed without question to what they wanted.

"Getting nervous?" Greg said once they were all assembled in the sanctuary.

"I wouldn't call it nervous. It's more like excited. I can hardly wait to make Jenny my wife and adopt Alex."

To Brand's surprise, big tears filled Alex's eyes and began running down his cheeks.

"What's wrong?" Brand got down on one knee to be on Alex's level.

"I want you to be my father, but if you adopt me, will I still be Chippewa?"

Brand's heart ached at the agony in Alex's question. "Nothing will ever make you anything but Chippewa. I want to adopt you so you will be my son and I will be your father. How would it be if when the time comes we talk to the judge and ask him if you can keep the last name of Red Hawk and still be adopted by me?"

A wide smile crossed Alex's lips. "I'd like that. Do you think I could be called Alex Red Hawk-Masterson? That way I could still be Chippewa and be your son, too."

The wisdom of this child was astonishing. The last thing he wanted to do was take away his heritage. "I think that's the best suggestion I've heard yet. I don't want to change either you or your mother in any way. I just want us to be a family."

Alex stepped forward and threw his arms around Brand's neck, "I'm so glad you love my mommy and want me to be your son."

* * * *

The soft beat of tribal drums mingled with the sound of the flutes signaled the beginning of Jenny and Brand's wedding. Jenny watched as first Frannie and then Leslie walked down the aisle of the church. They were dressed in traditional Chippewa clothing, and even though Frannie's long hair was blonde, she looked every inch the picture of a Chippewa princess.

Jenny smoothed down the skirt of her white doeskin dress. Her great-grandmother did the beading on the bodice for her grandmother's wedding over fifty years earlier. The suit worn by both her father and grandfather when they married into the family was in the same chest as the dress had been. Jenny could only imagine how Brand looked in the suit the men in her family had worn for generations.

Her father stepped up beside her and tucked her left arm into his right. "It's time, baby," he whispered. "You look as beautiful today as your mother did on the day we were married."

"Thank you. I hope Brand and I will be as happy as you and Mom have been all these years. You were a special man to take on a ready-made family, and I think Brand is just as special. Alex loves him as much as any little boy could ever love his father. I know it was the same between you and Matt."

"It was. I was so pleased when Matt's father gave up his rights so I could adopt him. Since Charlie doesn't acknowledge Alex as his son, the way is clear for Brand to adopt Alex. Do you think that's his plan?"

"I know it is. He wants to be Alex's father. After today, things will be easier for him to do that."

The music changed, and the congregation rose to its feet in preparation for Jenny to walk down the aisle toward her future. As she made her way toward Brand's side, she saw all the people who had been special in her life as well as those who were special to Brand. In the front pew, right behind her mother, was Ben Little Horse. He beamed as though she was his daughter rather than the woman who had given birth to the grandson he hadn't been able to acknowledge publicly until recently.

Just before she reached the place where Brand and Alex waited for her, Alex stepped forward to take his place on her right side and finish walking her forward to where Brand waited.

Whatever the minister said, was lost to Jenny. All she heard were the words of the vows that Brand had written especially for today. "I, Brand, take you, Jennifer, to be my wife. I also take Alexander as my son. I love you both more than life itself and promise to continue to love you for the remainder of my life. For better or worse, richer or poorer, in sickness and in health, I will be there for you. For this, I give you my heart as well as my name."

Jenny held Brand's hand a little tighter, as she repeated the vows she had written. "I, Jennifer, take you, Brandon, as my husband. You have made my life complete and together we will face any storms that life may give us. On behalf of both my son and myself, I say my vows with love. For better or worse, richer or poorer, in sickness and in health, I will be there for you. For this, I give you my heart and take your name with pride."

Within a matter of minutes, the rings were exchanged and the minister proclaimed them husband and wife. After Brand took her in his arms and kissed her for the first time, as his wife, they turned to face their guests. Amid applause from the congregation, they hurried down the aisle where they embraced and again kissed.

"I love you, Jenny Masterson," Brand said. "I can hardly wait for the wedding night so we can start working on the family we both want."

Chapter Sixteen

Lac Du Flambeau Reservation April 2009

Jenny Masterson rubbed the small of her back. This pregnancy was taking a lot out of her. Unlike her other two pregnancies, she found she tired much easier. It was probably because they were anxiously awaiting the birth of their twin daughters in two months. Alex, now ten, was thrilled with the prospect of having twin sisters in addition to his two-year-old brother, Austin.

She couldn't ask for a better big brother for her children than her oldest son. She'd been thrilled with the fact Alex enjoyed his role and never tired of the questions a two-year-old asked.

"Are you ready to head for home?" Brand said as he came up behind her.

"More than ready. What do you say we stop off and pick up one of those take-and-bake pizzas for supper? I'm pooped."

"I'm way ahead of you. I called over and ordered it so all we have to do is pick it up and not have to wait. I think it's time for you to take your maternity leave. You're exhausted. I don't want to put either you or our babies in jeopardy."

"Is this my doctor or my husband speaking?"

"Both. I talked it over with your OB-GYN, and she agrees with me. We can talk to the head of nursing tomorrow and see how soon we can arrange for you to be gone until six weeks after the girls are born. Then if you decide to go back to work, so be it, but you have to know it's not necessary."

"I do and you know I appreciate it immensely. What kind of pizza did you order?"

"The kind we all like — Canadian bacon, pineapple, and green olives."

Jenny knew the green olives were added for her, since she'd been craving them ever since she got pregnant. Brand had turned both her and Alex onto Hawaiian pizza when they were first married. She especially enjoyed it when she was pregnant because the green peppers she loved on her pizzas tended to talk back to her.

After stopping for the pizza, they went her parent's house next door to theirs where Alex and two-year old-Austin waited for them. The expression on her mother's face was one of concern. Jenny knew it was because her mother didn't approve of her working when it tired her so much.

"Are you all right, honey?" her mother said, as soon as they got out of the car.

"I'm fine, just a little tired is all. We stopped and picked up a take and bake pizza."

"You know you'd be welcome to have dinner with us tonight."

"I know but we have something we have to talk over with Alex and Austin," Brand replied. "Jenny has decided to start her maternity leave sooner than she did with Austin. The twins are taking a lot out of her, and she wants to know how Alex would like a full time mommy?"

"Really?" Alex said. "Are you really going to stay home all day?"

Jenny smiled. "I'm giving my notice tomorrow, and after next week, I'll be a full time mommy. For now, we have a great pizza just waiting to be slipped in the oven and baked. Do you think you can help me with it?"

The look on Alex's face was one of excitement. More than anything else, her son loved to work in the kitchen with her. Ever since he was little, he'd been setting the table for his grandmother, and now he took over the same job for his parents. He also loved helping cook. Often on Saturday morning, she and Brand would wake to the smell of bacon frying as Alex fixed them breakfast in bed.

* * * *

They'd just finished eating and she lowered herself into the recliner to kick back and watch television when the phone rang.

"Hello," Jenny answered.

"I have a collect call for you from Charlie Little Horse," the operator said in greeting. "Will you accept the charges?"

Jenny's hands trembled and her stomach clenched. "No, I won't," she replied, her tone a mixture of hatred and anger.

"Are you certain?" the operator pressed.

"Positive. I will take no calls from Mr. Little Horse now or any time in the future." With that said, she slammed down the receiver.

"Is something wrong, honey?" Brand said when he came back into the living room.

"Charlie just called me collect. Did he think I'd really accept the charges?"

"You didn't, did you?"

"No way. What could he possibly want? It's been four years. Does he think I could possibly want anything to do with him after everything he's done to me? Doesn't he realize what the papers he signed giving up his parental rights to Alex meant?"

"I'm sure he does, but he's been in prison for the last four years. Maybe he's changed. He is Alex's biological father."

"I don't want him to be my father," Alex said as he came into the room. "You're my father, not some criminal."

Jenny was horrified to think Alex overheard their conversation, yet they hadn't been whispering. He knew about Charlie's involvement in their lives and why he'd been sent to prison. Alex also knew Ben as his biological grandfather who loved him without reservation. She'd done everything in her power so his biological father's family got to see him often, even though Ben had been receptive when Brand wanted to start adoption proceedings she knew it bothered him having his grandson carry Brand's name.

Before either of them could comment on what Alex said, the phone rang again. This time Brand answered.

"Hello."

Jenny's heart pounded wildly as she listened to Brand's end of the conversation.

"Yes Ben, we got a collect call from Charlie."

Jenny's breathing returned to normal. Ben wasn't out to hurt them. Without listening further, she pulled Alex into her arms and assured her son of the love she and Brand had for him.

"We need to talk, and I mean all of us," Brand said once he ended his conversation. "This concerns you, too, Alex."

Jenny's apprehension returned. "What did Ben have to say?"

Brand seated himself on the couch and motioned for Alex to come and sit beside him. "You know Charlie Little Horse is your biological father and Ben is your paternal grandfather. I'm your father by my choice, and Ben has agreed with my adoption of you."

"I don't want Charlie to be my father."

"I know you don't, but we have to settle some things. Charlie is being released from prison next week, and he wants to come back to this area."

"He can't. He can't do this to us," Jenny protested.

"He can, and it's what he's planning to do. Because of his heritage, he has every right to come back here. What we have to decide is how we're going to handle it. What Ben suggested was getting a restraining order against him. That way he can't come anywhere near us. Since he never supported you or Alex, Ben asked Charlie to terminate his rights when he helped us with the adoption. If he hadn't signed the papers Ben took to the prison, I couldn't have adopted Alex."

"I don't want him anywhere near me," Alex proclaimed. "He's not my father."

"Not legally, but biologically he is," Brand explained. "Once we get the restraining order, he'll be restricted from coming anywhere near us. We'll be just fine."

Jenny prayed what Brand told them was true. In no way did she want Charlie anywhere near Alex. Father or no father, he had no right. As far as she was concerned on the day she told him she was pregnant, he'd given up any rights he had to her son. Four years ago he'd called Alex her bastard. How could he even consider returning to the reservation and insisting he had any rights to a son he never wanted?

"Will he really stay away from us," Alex asked. "The kids at school say he's bad news."

Jenny and Brand exchanged worried glances. "How do the kids at school know about Charlie?" Brand said.

"John Black Bear told me his father and Charlie were good friends in high school. He said I was Charlie's bastard kid and that Charlie was bad news."

"What did you say back to him?" Jenny studied her son.

"I told him he wasn't telling me anything I didn't know, and Charlie never wanted me, so Grandpa Little Horse made it okay for Brand to be my adopted father. He started calling me a bastard and got the big kids at school to call me the same thing."

Although Jenny never wanted anything as ugly as the word bastard to be associated with her son, the ugly truth about his conception had finally come out.

"Do you know what a bastard is?" Brand said.

Alex nodded. "It's a kid who doesn't have a father. When they call me names, I just tell them I have a father just not the one who made me. I tell them my father is someone who wants to be with me and made sure I'd be his for the rest of my life."

Jenny wanted to cry at the simplicity of her son's answer. When they went through the adoption proceedings, those were the things Brand told Alex. At the time, she didn't think he really understood what had been happening.

"What do you know about how babies are made?" Brand continued.

Alex rolled his eyes. "Ah, Dad, you know we talked about those things when Mom got pregnant with Austin. I know what happens between boys and girls. We even had the talk about it in health class. When they talked about boys wearing condoms when they were with girls, they all were excited. I told them better condoms were all right, but not for me. I said my dad waited for the right girl to be with forever, and I wanted to do the same. They all laughed at me."

Jenny pulled Alex into her arms. "It's hard for kids to understand what you just said when everything they see on television and hear in the songs on the radio says sex before marriage is acceptable."

"Your mom's right," Brand agreed. "Peer pressure can be rough when it comes to sex before marriage. I should know. I went through it when I was a kid. Everyone told me I was a wuss for wanting to wait. When I met your mom, I knew I'd found the one woman worth waiting for. You will be too, but I'm not saying it won't be hard."

Alex hugged them both tightly before going to bed. Jenny knew her son was convinced, no matter what, she and Brand would protect him with their lives if need be. She prayed the time wouldn't come when they would have to lay their lives on the line, but with Charlie coming home soon, it looked as though it might become a distinct possibility.

Chapter Seventeen

The alarm in Brand and Jenny's bedroom signaled it was time to rise. At least she had today off. After last night, neither of them slept much. Knowing within a week, they would be faced with Charlie living on the reservation full time, kept sleep at bay.

"You sleep," Brand whispered to her, as he got out of bed. "I'll take care of breakfast as well as getting your mother to come over and watch Austin. I'll also make sure Alex gets to school on time."

"But I have to talk to the head of nursing today, and we have to go to the police department for the restraining order."

"We can do everything later. You need your rest more than we need to do all this paperwork. I'll call you at noon, and we can have lunch together. Since it's Wednesday, I don't have office hours this afternoon. We can take care of everything then."

Jenny nodded and turned over, hugging her pillow tightly, the way he'd seen her do so many times before. When her breathing indicated she returned to sleep, he left the room and went into the bathroom for a much needed shower.

By six thirty, he had showered, shaved, and was heading for Alex's bedroom. To his surprise, Alex was already awake and dressed for school.

"I didn't think you'd be awake so early," Brand said.

"I didn't sleep much last night. Do you think my real dad will come here and make trouble for us?"

Brand sat down on the bed and motioned for Alex to join him. "Not if I can help it. Your mom and I are going to the police department today and get a restraining order against him. I'm sorry you didn't sleep much last night, but neither did your mom. I'm letting her sleep in this morning. Let's go down and fix a manly breakfast and then go across the driveway and see if your grandma can come over to take care of Austin when he wakes."

"You go over to Grandma and Grandpa's, and I'll start making breakfast for us."

Brand smiled at Alex. He was so proud of the boy it wasn't funny. If he could have ordered a perfect son, it would have been Alex. Rather than standing, he pulled the boy into his embrace. "Don't worry. We'll get past this. I'm not very hungry. Toast and coffee will be enough this morning."

Alex nodded against Brand's chest before wiggling out of his arms. "We'd better get going or we'll be late."

Brand glanced at the clock. It was already seven. They would have to hurry to have Alex to school by seven forty-five and still be at his office by eight.

While Alex made coffee and put the bread into the toaster, Brand went next door. It didn't surprise him to find Betsy sitting at her kitchen table sipping a cup of coffee.

"Can you could come over and keep an eye on Jenny and Austin this morning?" he said, when he entered the kitchen.

"Is something wrong?"

"I'm afraid there is. Charlie called Jenny collect from prison last night. She didn't accept the charges, but it wasn't long before we had a call from Ben. He told me he'd heard from Charlie, and he's being released from prison next week."

"Oh dear Lord, no. I thought he had he still had time left on his sentence."

"I did too, but Ben said he's getting out for good behavior. It didn't help matters when Jenny didn't accept the charges for his call. I'm not too proud to say I'm worried. None of us got a lot of sleep last night. I told her to sleep in and I'd see if you could come over and take care of Austin."

"What about Alex?"

"He's worried. I left him fixing my breakfast, so I need to get back. I have to get him to school. I only have a half a day today, so Jenny is meeting me for lunch. After that we're going to set up her maternity leave and go to the police station to get a restraining order against Charlie."

Betsy nodded and got to her feet. "You go ahead. I'll be right over. I just need to put these dishes in the sink."

Alex waited for Brand in the kitchen, a worried expression on his face.

"What's wrong," Brand asked.

"There was a phone call while you were over at Grandma's."

"Is it someone I need to call back?"

"No, Dad, it was a collect call from Charlie at the state prison. I answered it on the first ring so it wouldn't bother Mom."

"Oh dear God. Did you accept the charges?"

"No, but I could hear someone swearing in the background. I got scared and hung up the phone."

"You did the right thing. After your mom and I finish at the police station, we'll stop at the phone company and have our number changed to an unlisted one. Until I get it set, you're not to answer the phone. I'll go up and tell your mother what happened as soon as we finish our breakfast."

"If we get an unlisted number, how will my friends get in touch with me?"

"Once we get past this, we'll talk about getting you a cell phone so you can call your friends. For now, we'll deal with one problem at a time."

Alex seemed to accept what Brand told him, but the fear remained in his eyes. As soon as Betsy came to the house, Brand went upstairs to tell Jenny about the phone call Alex intercepted. His own fears mirrored those of his son. Even if changing their phone number stopped the phone calls for the time being, Charlie would be back in the area in a week. He prayed the restraining order they planned to get today would keep them safe.

* * * *

Ben Little Horse waited for Brand at the clinic. "I'm sorry about what happened last night," he said, as he followed Brand past the reception desk and into his office.

"You had nothing to do with it. I should have made our phone number unlisted years ago, but I never thought Charlie would track us down and try to call Jenny. To be truthful, he tried again this morning. This time Alex answered the phone. I was next door asking Betsy to come and watch

Austin while Jenny caught up on her sleep. This pregnancy is taking a lot out of her, and Charlie's call only added to the stress."

"My God, did Alex talk to Charlie?"

"Alex didn't accept the charges. Since today is only a half-day for me, I'm meeting Jenny for lunch. After we eat, we're going to get the paperwork started for her maternity leave, get that restraining order we talked about last night and change our phone to an unlisted number. Alex is worried about being able to talk to his friends, but until we know who's been in contact with Charlie while he's been in prison, I don't want to take any chances."

"I agree. I thought I knew what was going on in Charlie's mind. We've talked about him coming back here when he's released. He knows he has no right to Alex. He should for God's sake. He signed the papers giving up his rights when you wanted to adopt the boy. At the time, he told me he never did believe Alex was his son. On the other hand, I had no doubts. He looks so much like Charlie when he was a kid it's uncanny. Even when he was just a baby there was no doubt as to who fathered him."

Brand nodded. Even if Alex didn't look a thing like Charlie, he couldn't fault Ben for thinking his grandson was the spitting image of his son. Looking down he saw a white envelope on the floor of his office. Once Ben was seated in front of the desk, Brand bent down and retrieved the envelope before seating himself behind the desk facing Ben.

"What's that?" Ben asked.

"I have no idea. There's only one what to find out, though." Brand reached for the letter opener resting in the leather pencil holder on the far corner of his desk pad.

When he pulled out the piece of white paper that had been folded in half, he could hardly believe what it said. The words had been cut from newspapers as well as magazines and could be considered a threat.

"What does it say?" Ben reached for the note.

"It's disturbing," Brand replied as he handed the note to Ben. The words were seared into his mind and were something he would never forget.

You don't belong here White Eyes. Take your son and leave Jenny and Alex with their own people or you will seal your fate.

"Who could have sent you something like this?" Ben looked stunned. "My God, you've been at this hospital for four years and there's never been a problem."

"Not until now. I know I'm different from the people who live here, but I care for them regardless of our skin color. I've only been called White Eyes once in all that time and that was by your son, the night he assaulted Jenny. He's behind this although I don't know how he managed to get this to me when he's still in jail."

"Charlie has a lot of hatred in his heart. I think secretly he still loves Jenny. When she first told him she was going to have his baby, he didn't want to take the responsibility. To be truthful, I knew she'd told him when he was getting ready to go to college. Secretly I applauded him for going on to school rather than throw everything away because Jenny was going to have his child. I thought if I helped Jenny out financially, it would make up for Charlie not being here for her. Maybe if I had made him stand up and be a man back then, he wouldn't have gone bad."

"Hindsight is always 20/20, Ben. What was done in the past can't be changed, but I can't ignore this threat. I also can't let Jenny know about this."

"I'm afraid you'll have to tell her. She's in as much danger as you are. If this came from Charlie, I think I know what's prompting it."

"What do you mean?"

"Right after he went to back to prison after that business between him and Jenny, he was in a fight. To make a long story short, he was hurt badly enough that he can't father children. Unless there are others we don't know about, Alex is the only child he will ever have. He's seeing the future and doesn't like the way it looks. I think it would be wise if you sent Jenny and the kids away for a while."

"There's only one problem with that. Jenny is due to have the twins in two months. There's no way I can send her away from her doctor at this point. The place to start is by calling the police in on this one. I'm sorry to have to do this, considering how good you've been to us over the years, but I don't have any other options at this point."

"This has nothing to do with me, but it has everything to do with your family. I want you to be safe."

A Father's Love

Even though Ben said the words, Brand could tell all of this was taking its toll on his friend. He hadn't considered Ben to be an old man, but this new information about the danger threatening not only Brand but also Jenny and Alex had aged the man visibly.

Instead of calling Jenny and upsetting her with this latest development, Brand waited until Ben left his office before placing a call to the police department. Once assured the authorities were on their way, he buzzed his nurse and asked her to clear his calendar. In an emergency, there were others who could see his patients. This was a time when he needed to care for his own family. This threat could hurt Jenny and prove dangerous for their children as well as him.

It took only a few minutes for Officer Russell Eagle to arrive and to take a statement from Brand.

"Do you have any idea who sent this letter?" the officer said, taking the letter from Brand with gloved hands.

"I don't like to think about it, but Charlie Little Horse is Alex's natural father, and he's due to be released from prison next weekend. I can't help but believe he's behind this, I just don't know how he could have slipped the note under my office door while he's still an inmate in the state prison."

"Do you know anyone who could have been in contact with Charlie?"

Brand thought for a moment. Last night, Alex talked about John Black Bear being one of his tormentors at school. "My son told me John Black Bear has been calling him names. I asked why the boy would do such a thing, and he said John's father was a good friend of Charlie's. It's possible he's been in contact with Charlie, but I can't imagine Pete being behind this. He's been my patient for the last four years, and I thought we were friends. Other than that, I don't have any ideas. I never really knew Charlie or any of his friends, but he has to have someone on the reservation helping him get to Jenny."

"What do you mean?"

"Last night Jenny got a collect call from Charlie. She didn't accept the charges, but while I was getting Betsy to come over and take care of Austin so Jenny could sleep this morning, Alex got a collect call from him as well. He didn't accept the charges either, but Jenny and I planned to

139

come to the station this afternoon to get a restraining order against Charlie once he's released."

"This information gives me something to work with. I went to school with Jenny and Charlie. I ran with the same crowd as Charlie. I agree with you, about Pete, but there are several others who could be involved. I'll get that restraining order in place and check to see who has been to visit Charlie in the past week."

* * * *

Jenny awoke to the sun shining brightly through her bedroom window. After last night, she vaguely remembered Brand telling her to sleep in, but she never expected to sleep until after ten.

After dressing, the aroma of fresh coffee drew her toward the kitchen.

"Good morning, sleepy head," her mother greeted her. "Did you get some quality rest after Brand left?"

"I slept, but I experienced some terrible dreams. I don't want Charlie coming back here after he's released next week. He didn't want anything to do with Alex before he was born or after, but something tells me he's going to try to see him once he gets home. I can't allow that. Brand is his father by choice. He's wanted him from day one. He's—"

"Listen to yourself, honey," her mother interrupted. "No one doubts the way Brand feels about Alex. Trust me. He won't let anything happen to either one of you."

Before Jenny could respond, the phone rang. After checking the caller ID and seeing the number for the grade school, she answered.

"Mrs. Masterson, this is Alex's teacher, Carolyn Hunter. We have a bit of a problem."

"A problem? What kind of a problem?"

"We were on a nature walk, and when we got back to the school, Alex was missing. I talked to some of his friends, but they said they became separated when we were in the woods. I've called the police, and they're searching for him, but I wanted to let you know."

"Have you called my husband?"

"He's a doctor, and I didn't want to bother him."

"What do you mean you didn't want to bother him?"

"It isn't like he's actually the boy's father and—"

"And nothing. I'll call him myself." She slammed down the receiver, angry to hear the teacher say such a thing.

Everyone on the reservation knew Brand adopted Alex. There were some who resented a white main adopting a Chippewa child, but never before had they said such a thing to her.

She took a deep breath to calm her nerves before turning to face her mother. As she did, she heard sirens coming toward the house. Before she could get to her feet the noise stopped, and Brand rushed into the house.

"Thank God you're all right."

"Oh Brand, I just got a call from school. Alex is missing."

"I know. I received a threatening note at work and called the police in on it. Russ arrived at the office, and we were discussing it when he received the call about Alex. Considering the content of the note, we decided to get over here and make certain you weren't in any danger."

"Me? What did the note say? Let me see it."

"I'm afraid we can't let you see it, Jenny," Russ said, as he entered the kitchen. "I put it in an evidence bag so our lab can analyze it. With luck, we can lift some fingerprints from either the envelope or the letter or better yet some DNA from the envelope flap where it was licked shut. I can tell you what it said. Basically, it indicated Brand didn't belong here and called him White Eyes. The remainder of the note advised him to take Austin and leave the reservation."

"What about me?" She sank down on to one of the kitchen chairs.

"It said you and Alex belonged here and should stay, honey," Brand replied. "I'm sure Charlie has something to do with all of this. When I found it, Ben was waiting for me. He told me Charlie was in a fight in prison, and he's no longer able to father children. Alex will always be his only child, unless, of course, there were other women who never came forward to accuse him of fathering their kids."

"Charlie has a terrible temper, but I can't believe he's behind this. How could he put his own child in danger? Besides, he's not going to be released from prison until next week. He couldn't possibly be in on this."

Before anyone could say anything, Russ' cell phone rang. He stepped from the room, for privacy giving Brand, Jenny, and Betsy some time alone.

"Where's Austin?" Brand said.

"I put him down for a nap about fifteen minutes ago," Betsy responded.

"That's a relief. I'm afraid we're all in danger. Charlie has a long reach."

"Are you sure Charlie is involved in this?" Betsy looked doubtful.

Brand nodded. "I've been on this reservation for four years, and in all that time there was only one person who ever called me White Eyes and that was Charlie. That was the name mentioned in the note. He has to be behind this."

"Don't jump to too many conclusions, Brand," Russ said, as he entered the room.

"What?" Brand demanded.

"I just talked to the commander at the station, and he's been in touch with the prison. In the past two months, Charlie hasn't had any visitors, he hasn't corresponded with anyone, and the only phone calls he's made have been to his father as well as the two calls he tried to place to you. There's no way he could be involved in this."

"Then who?"

"It could be anyone, even you."

Jenny's world began to collapse around her. How could anyone suspect Brand? He loved his children, Alex included.

"That's crazy, Russ. Brand wouldn't do anything to harm Alex."

"Look Jenny, I know that and so do you, but he's the one who got the note. From what Brand told me, he found it in his office. Someone shoved it under his door sometime before he got there. He could have put it there last night before he went home. Then there's Ben. He was waiting for Brand this morning. He could have put it under the door. Until we can rule them out, everyone is suspect."

Jenny thought of all the cop shows she and Brand enjoyed watching. They always suspected the people closest to the victims, but to suspect Brand or even Ben was completely out of the question.

"Brand could easily want to be shed of his adopted child now he has a family of his own," Russ said. "Ben could want Alex all to himself, since Charlie can no longer have children."

"What do you mean Charlie can't have children?"

Brand sat down next to Jenny and took her hand in his. "This morning Ben told me after Charlie went back to prison he was in a fight and got cut badly enough he can't father children any longer. Ben will never have a grandson to carry on his family name. He could easily be behind Alex's kidnapping so he could legally change his name to Little Horse."

Jenny shook her head in disbelief. "I can't imagine Ben doing something like that." Even as she said the words, doubts assailed her.

Her mind swirled so fast she could hardly process the information. As she thought about the events of the morning, the image of Brand's face when Russ accused him filled her mind. Brand showed no outrage at the accusation. Why wasn't he screaming his innocence at the top of his lungs?

Emotions in a turmoil, Jenny didn't know what to think or whom to believe. Even though she didn't want to believe anyone in the police department would accuse her husband, she still had to ask the question. "Are you responsible for this?"

Brand tightened his grip on Jenny's hand, but she could hardly stand his touch. "I wasn't surprised because Russ and I talked about this on the way over. I understand family is suspected in anything like this, and I also know my fingerprints are all over the note. That being the case, I probably obliterated any viable prints. As for Ben, it's a possibility, but I doubt it. When I opened the note the shock on his face was evident, at least it was to me. If he is involved, he's one hell of an actor."

"No matter what he says, we're taking him down to the station for questioning," Russ said. "I'm afraid you'll have to come along with me was well, Brand. I can't leave any lead unexplored."

Jenny couldn't believe any of this was happening. Alex couldn't be missing, and even if he was, Brand couldn't be responsible. She got to her feet and as she did, she felt the babies drop into position as the first pains of labor hit. With one hand on her stomach and the other reaching out to Brand, she collapsed against her husband for support.

"This can't be happening," she moaned. "I can't be in labor."

"I'm afraid you are. Can you give us a ride to the hospital to get Jenny checked out, Russ? Once I'm certain she's all right, I promise I'll come down to the station and give a statement."

Between Russ and Brand, they guided Jenny out of the house and helped settle her in the back of the squad car. As soon as Brand slid into the back seat beside her, Russ brought the engine to life and hit the siren as they headed toward the hospital.

Even though Brand put his arm around her shoulders and pulled her against him for support, the look on his face when Russ first accused him kept flashing before her eyes. She'd been outraged, but Brand acted as though the accusation came as no surprise.

Another pain cut through her belly. It couldn't have been any more than ten minutes after the first one hit. The stress of the day brought everything on early. By tonight it was possible the twins would be born and fighting for their lives as preemies. In her mind, she couldn't stop the thoughts of Brand bringing all of this on. Was it possible he no longer wanted to be Alex's father? Was this his way of getting out of a situation he considered unbearable? She knew her negative ramblings were only because of the stress of her pregnancy and the early labor. She loved Brand and knew he would never do anything to hurt any of them.

After seating her in the wheelchair the emergency room orderlies were holding, they rushed her into an examination room. To her surprise, her OBGYN doctor waited for her.

"I'm going to examine Jenny, Brand, so you'll have to wait until we call you."

Jenny breathed a sigh of relief the moment Brand left the examination room.

"What's going on Jenny?" Dr. Bryant said. "I know about Alex being missing, but you act as though you're scared to death of Brand."

"I am, I'm not, I don't know how I feel right now other than frightened for these babies as well as Alex. Russ brought him to the house and then said he was a suspect. I have every right to be scared. What if he no longer wants to be Alex's father? What if Charlie was right when he called him a 'white eyes'? What if he really doesn't want to be with us? He's the father of my son as well as these twins. I love him so much, but at the same time I'm scared to death of him."

"That's because you're in active labor," Dr. Bryant said once she finished her examination. "You're dilated to eight. We have just enough

A Father's Love

time to get you up to the delivery room. I don't want to deliver twins in the emergency department."

Jenny lay back on the gurney as they pushed her out of the examination room and into the hallway on the way to the delivery room. Brand waited for her and immediately took her hand in his. Instead of feeling secure and loved by his touch, she tensed, intensifying the next labor pain to cut through her body.

* * * *

Brand felt the tension in Jenny's hand. It was ridiculous for anyone even to consider him as having anything to do with Alex's disappearance, but Russ' accusations brought on not only Jenny's labor, but also the fear he felt radiating toward him.

Russ waited for them just outside the emergency department and went with them to the delivery room. It was one thing to have a police escort to the hospital, but for Russ to be sticking to them like glue even as they went upstairs for the delivery of their twins was something else. More and more Brand was beginning to feel like a suspect rather than the father of a missing child.

Within an hour, Anna and Amy were born, both weighing just under five pounds but perfect in every other way. As a precaution, they were whisked away to the nursery where matching incubators waited for them. Russ allowed him to stay with Jenny until she was in a room and then insisted Brand accompany him to the police station.

"I've watched enough cop shows on TV to understand why you have to suspect everyone, but aren't you carrying this a bit too far? I'm not responsible for my son's disappearance. Why waste time with me when you could be out there looking for the man who actually took him?"

"There are plenty of officers out looking for Alex. I have to check out every lead. To be truthful, you'd have a lot to gain by throwing the blame on Charlie. For all I know, you want out of here. It can't be easy being in the minority. You don't have many white patients, and the people you see and work with every day aren't of the upper middle class. You could be making a hell of a lot more money somewhere else. Of course, with an Indian wife and kid, to say nothing about three half-breeds, life wouldn't be easy for you anywhere other than this reservation."

145

Brand would have given anything not to be in the backseat of a police cruiser accused of something so absurd he could hardly comprehend it. If there weren't a wire mesh separating him from Russ, he would have gladly wrung the man's neck.

At the station, Brand allowed Russ to fingerprint him before taking him to an interrogation room. Although he expected Russ to come in to question him, it came as a surprise when a man he didn't know came into the room.

"I'm Agent Samuel Cullen of the FBI in Minneapolis, Dr. Masterson," the man said extending his hand toward Brand. "We've checked the note you received this morning and the only fingerprints on it belong to you and Ben Little Horse. Do you have any explanation for that?"

"Of course I do. I opened the envelope, I read the note, and I handed it to Ben to read. I'm not surprised to have my fingerprints on that paper. I'd be surprised if they weren't. What are you getting at?"

"I'd expect to find the prints of the man who put the note under your door. Everyone knows you adopted Jenny Red Hawk's son, why did you do that?"

The question caught Brand completely off guard. "To begin with, if I wanted to send a threatening note to someone, I'd use gloves so my fingerprints wouldn't show. As for why I adopted Alex, I did so because I love him like my own. I knew coming into this he and Jenny were a package deal."

"That might have been the way things looked when you got married, but since then you've had another son, and I've been told your wife just gave birth to twin daughters. Things change. It's possible you'd be happier if you didn't have a Chippewa son in the mix."

The statement outraged Brand more than even the ride in the police cruiser. "That's the most asinine thing I've ever heard. I love Alex in the same way as I love Austin and as I will love the twins. Even though I'm not his natural father, I can't imagine life without him."

"Those are big words, but I doubt their sincerity. If I had an Indian wife with an Indian son, I'd resent him taking the place of my own blood. In my heart, he would always be the outsider in our family. Something tells me deep in your heart you feel the same way about Alex."

"Look you don't know me, and as far as I'm concerned you have no right to judge me. I love my son. I certainly wouldn't have him kidnapped. I'm sure Charlie Little Horse is behind this."

"That's where you're wrong. Since Charlie was going to be released next week, we were able to bring him home today. He wants to search for his son."

"He gave up his rights to Alex four years ago when he signed the papers so I could adopt the boy. I can't believe you brought him here."

Agent Cullen looked up at the one-way mirror on the wall and motioned to the unseen person behind the glass. Several seconds later, the door opened and a man entered. Even though Brand only saw Charlie once, he would have known him anywhere. Prison hadn't been easy on him, and he'd aged far beyond his twenty-eight years, but he was still the Charlie Little Horse Brand remembered.

"We meet again, White Eyes," Charlie said as he entered the room.

"I can't say it's good to see you, Charlie," Brand replied. "I thought Jenny made it clear she didn't want to talk to you when she didn't accept the charges to you call last night."

"She did, but she needs to hear what I have to say."

"And just what would that be?"

"I've never admitted to anyone what everyone knew was the truth. Alex is my son, even though I gave up my rights to him. I couldn't be a father to him in prison. Even so, I realized I wanted to be close enough to watch him grow and maybe be a friend to him. From what my father said, you've been good to the boy, so why would you kidnap him now?"

"I didn't. I thought you were behind this."

Charlie shook his head and then sat down across the table from Brand. "For the past four years I've wanted to hate you, but my father has great respect for you. The officers here, as well as the FBI agent all told me they think either you or my father did this because your fingerprints are all over the note you received in your office."

"And you believe them?"

"I wanted to, God knows I wanted to. I just left my father. They've been questioning him as well. I'm afraid he's a broken man. He can't believe he was brought in for questioning, and to be truthful, neither can I.

I also don't believe you would take care of my son for four years like he was your own and suddenly turn on him."

"So who do you think has Alex?"

"We have to go along with the cops until they can prove your innocence."

"What happened to innocent until proven guilty?" Brand demanded.

"I'm probably a bit cynical, but being an ex-con I have every right to be. I met more people in prison who said they were innocent than ones who admitted to being guilty. None of it matters now. If I had to make a guess who's behind this, I'd put my money on Preston Silver Wolf. I have a sinking feeling he could have the boy."

"Who's this Preston Silver Wolf, and why haven't I heard the family name before," Brand asked.

"He was my cellmate for the first couple of years I was in prison. I was bitter back then, and I wanted to hurt not only you but also Jenny. I talked about how my dad was a wealthy man and believed Alex was his grandson. If I'm not mistaken, he's taken the boy to get money from my dad. As for why you haven't heard of him, his folks are from Minnesota. His dad is Sioux, and his mother is white."

"What was he in prison for? If he is the kidnaper, is Alex in any danger?"

"I don't think he's violent, if that's what you mean. From what he told me, he's been involved in petty theft since he was a kid. Unfortunately, he graduated to auto theft and the rest as they say is history. He has no idea how to earn an honest living. I'm certain he'll contact my dad for a ransom. I suggested the police have dad's phone transferred here so when he gets the call it can be monitored."

"And me? Don't you think this man might not contact our house for a ransom?"

"Probably not. I didn't speak highly of you. He sent you a note as a warning of what might happen. I think he has some warped idea since I'm supposed to be getting out next week I'd appreciate having my son back."

"And would you?"

Charlie shook his head. "I have no claim to the boy. I never did. I was a fool to deny him, but I'm the first to admit I was glad when the old man came to me and asked me to sign away my rights. From everything I've

148

heard, Alex is a good kid, and he deserves to have a father he can respect. He certainly doesn't need an ex-con coming into his life at this point and claiming to be his father."

"But you're planning to come back here."

"Where else can I go? I didn't do well in the outside world, and my dad told me there's a place for me at the plant. He's promised my sister and her husband they'll inherit everything. They've earned the right. I just want a place to live, a job to do, and a chance to make amends for the things I've done to shame my family in the past. Hell, I couldn't even go to my own mother's funeral. I think the only reason Dad has anything to do with me over the past four years is because he promised her he wouldn't give up on his only son."

"That's all fine and good, Charlie," Agent Cullen interrupted, "but the fact is the only fingerprints on the note come from your father and Dr. Masterson. They're the logical suspects and the people with the most to gain."

"How do you figure that?" Brand demanded.

The agent looked at Brand as though he had no right to ask such a question. "To begin with, you now have a natural son and twin daughters. What kind of a man wants to raise another man's child?"

"This kind of a man," Brand shouted. "I love Alex like he's my own. There's no way I would ever want him out of my life, to say nothing of what you're thinking."

"I'm interested to know what makes you suspect my dad," Charlie said.

"With you coming back, maybe the old man had a change of mind. If I can believe what we've been told, you can't father another child. Alex is his only chance for a grandson to carry on his name. Your sister's kids don't have Little Horse as their last name."

"That's a bunch of bull, and you know it," Charlie responded. "I'm betting my money on Preston. He's the only logical choice. He thinks he can get money from my old man. Considering the son-of-a-bitch hasn't ever worked a day in his life has to count for something. I was pretty pissed back when we were cellmates, and I made no bones about the old man being loaded or how much I hated Jenny for marrying a white man and having my son brought up by someone who wasn't Chippewa."

"I thought you didn't consider Alex your son," Agent Cullen said.

"What I consider doesn't have anything to do with it. When Jenny told me she was pregnant, I knew the kid was mine. I just didn't want anything to screw up my future. I was going to go to college on a football scholarship, and I didn't want to be saddled with a wife and a brat to support. It was easier for me to say the kid wasn't mine. I even called him Jenny's bastard. Deep in my heart, I knew he was my kid. Hell, I was the only one ever to be with Jenny.

"Four years ago, I knew Jenny was going to the sledding party because I called and asked her to go with me and she turned me down. I'd come back to town and realized I loved her back in high school, probably still did. I'd heard she had some white guy staying at the house for the weekend, and I didn't like the idea of her being with someone who wasn't Chippewa. That's why I called Brand 'White Eyes' and why I assaulted Jenny. I paid for it with four years behind bars. I know now it was just my inflated ego. From everything I've heard, Brand is the best thing to have happened to both Jenny and Alex."

Agent Cullen shook his head as though completely bored with what seemed to be a change in Charlie's personality. "All of that is ancient history. None of it changes the fact the only prints on the note Dr. Masterson found in his office belong to him and your dad. For now, Dr. Masterson, you're fee to go, but don't leave town. The same goes for your father, Charlie."

Brand left the interrogation room in time to see Ben leave a similar room across the hall. For the first time, he thought of Ben as an older man. It was evident he'd aged at least ten years since their early morning meeting at the hospital.

Brand wondered if he had aged since he got Alex up for school this morning. Twelve hours earlier, they'd been a happy family, expecting the birth of the twins in two months. Tonight, Alex was missing. Jenny was in the hospital, and the twins were in incubators in the nursery at the hospital. To make matters worse, he was under suspicion for the kidnapping of his own son.

As much as he wanted to go home and stand under the shower for at least an hour to wash off the stink of the police department, he knew he had to go to the hospital to be with Jenny.

"Brand, what are you doing here?" Ben said as soon as their eyes made contact.

"The same thing as you, I guess. They think I'm behind this."

"I doubt they still think that. We just got a call for the ransom. The man said Alex is all right, but he wants two hundred thousand dollars by tomorrow morning."

The request didn't come as a shock. If the man Charlie suspected took Alex, it was possible he would ask for some outrageous amount of money as a ransom.

"How can we come up with so much money in such a short time?" Brand put emphasis on the word 'we'. "I can talk to my folks, but they don't have that kind of money at their fingertips."

"I can come up with at least half of it," Ben said. "The other half would be impossible."

Brand considered what he and Jenny had in the bank. With each paycheck, they put away money for the kids. Along with what his parents contributed, they now had twenty five hundred dollars each for Alex and Austin's educations. There was also the account Jenny kept from the money Ben gave Alex over the years. At the most, it contained another ten thousand, making the total twenty thousand. It was a long way from the hundred thousand they still needed. It was possible he could get another ten thousand from his father as well as his sisters and their husbands, but it still fell short by fifty thousand dollars.

"Where are you supposed to take the ransom?" Agent Cullen looked angry.

"The man asked for it to be left at the community center in a trash can, Sam," a woman Brand assumed to be another FBI agent said. "He also said he wanted Dr. Masterson to bring it at five tomorrow morning and to come alone."

Brand's mind ran wild. Even if his sisters and his parents were able to come up with the money, there was no way they could have it to him by early tomorrow morning. By this time, the banks would be closed and there would be no way to get the money before the appointed drop time.

"No one will have to come up with the money," Agent Cullen said. "We have money earmarked for such things. It's also marked, so if this guy tries to spend it, we'll know immediately. You'll have to be the one to deliver the money, Dr. Masterson."

Brand nodded. "I'll do anything to get my son back. Did they let you talk to him?"

Tears pooled in Ben's eyes. "No. He just said Alex was all right. He said I'd know what I needed to know once you delivered the money."

Brand's stomach began to sink. If the man hadn't allowed Ben to talk to Alex, it could mean anything. For all they knew, Alex was already dead. The very thought of such a thing made him want to vomit, even though he knew with nothing to eat since the toast and coffee he'd eaten early this morning, there would be nothing in his stomach to lose. With all of this happening today, there had been no time for lunch and now it was far past the dinner hour.

Chapter Eighteen

What should have been the happiest day of Jenny's life suddenly turned into her worst nightmare. Although her pediatrician assured her that other than being small, the twins were healthy, she still worried about how early they'd been born. Adding to her anxiety was Alex's disappearance and the fact Brand had to go down to the police station as soon as the girls were born.

"What's going on," she asked her father for the hundredth time.

"I wish I knew honey," Tom replied. "It's as though Alex has disappeared into thin air. I wanted to go out looking for him, but the police said you needed me more. They brought in the FBI this afternoon. There's nothing we can do that's not already being done."

As much as Jenny agonized over the safety of her son, she worried about her father as well. Last year he'd suffered a mild heart attack, and she feared another could be brought on by everything happening in their lives. As his first grandchild, Alex held a special place in Tom Red Hawk's heart. She could only pray his heart was strong enough to withstand things if the worst were to happen.

"I know I can't be out there looking for him," Jenny acknowledged. "What about Mom and Austin? Are they safe?"

"Russ assured me they have an officer at the house. From what I've heard about the contents of the note Brand received this morning, you and Alex were the primary targets. They have officers stationed outside your door as well as at the nursery."

"What about Brand? He was the one to get the note. I haven't seen him since Russ took him down to the station right after the girls were born. Why are they keeping him away from us?"

The look in her father's eyes told her what she didn't want to know. The police still considered Brand a suspect in Alex's disappearance. Could they be right? Was Brand fed up with being a father to another man's child? Since he hadn't returned from the police station, it was entirely possible.

"How's the prettiest mother in the world?" Brand said, drawing Jenny's attention toward the doorway where he stood.

"I'm tired, worried, scared, take your pick."

Brand crossed the room and took her hand in his. He put it to his mouth and kissed it. "I stopped off to see our beautiful daughters," he said. "Have you been down to see them?"

"They let the escort outside my door go down to the nursery with me about an hour ago. What took you so long to get back? They suspect you, don't they?"

Brand nodded. "At this point they suspect everyone, even Ben. However, they also have another suspect."

"What about Charlie? He's the one they should be questioning."

"They're convinced he had nothing to do with it. He thinks it's some guy who was his cellmate a couple of years ago and has been in contact with since the man was released. They let Charlie out early to help in the investigation as well as the search for Alex."

"That makes sense," Tom added. "I remember when the kids were little, a bunch of us guys worked with the boy scouts and taught them the art of tracking. Charlie was the best student we had. It was something I remember my dad teaching me, but it's almost a lost art. If anyone can track down Alex it will be Charlie."

"I don't want him anywhere near us," Jenny said.

"I didn't either, but I got a chance to talk to him. He told me the reason he called last night as well as this morning was to let you know he was coming home and he didn't want to interfere with our family. He wants to get to know Alex, but he doesn't want to be his father. It's hard to comprehend, but I believe him. He doesn't think I'm guilty, but the way it sounds he's in the minority where that's concerned."

"What about other leads?" Tom said, giving Jenny time to think about what Brand just told her.

"Just before I left the police station, they got a call from the kidnapper.

"A kidnapper?" Jenny looked aghast.

"Yes, he wants a ransom of two hundred thousand dollars delivered to the community center tomorrow morning at five. I'm supposed to deliver it and come alone."

"Do we have that kind of money," Jenny asked.

"If we had more time, between Ben and me we could have raised it. I had it figured out how we could come up with some of the money, and Ben said he could put his hands on a hundred thousand dollars right away, but it wasn't enough. The FBI says they have drop money available. We're going to use that."

"Do you think it's wise for you to do that?" Tom said.

"Probably not, but we haven't any other option. If this sick bastard wants me, I'm planning to be the one he gets. I'd give anything to get my hands around his neck and choke him until he tells me what I want to know. The problem is, the cops say I can't touch him or I'll put Alex in more danger than he's already in."

Jenny started to cry. "Do you really think he's still alive? I've watched enough shows on television to know kidnappers rarely return their victims alive. They kill them for the thrill and then ask for the ransom to give them money to get away. What if he's dead?"

"I don't think he'd dead and neither does Charlie. If it's the guy he thinks it is, he says he's into petty theft more than violent crimes. Charlie also thinks this guy only wants the money and is doing it so Charlie can get his son back."

"Then he does want to take Alex from me."

"From us," Brand corrected. "He told me he shared a cell with this man when he first went to prison, before he got in the fight that took away his ability to have more kids. Charlie's had a lot of time to think about what kind of a father Alex needs. He said he knows he's not father material and certainly not a great role model.

"Trust me, I love Alex with all my heart, and I believe Charlie when he says he wouldn't harm him. My prayer is we catch this monster before he hurts our son."

Jenny's prayers echoed those of her husband. She was relieved to know even though the authorities thought Brand was involved, everything he told her eased her mind about the man she loved more than anything else in the world.

* * * *

Visiting hours were over far too soon for Brand's liking, but Jenny needed her rest. When Tom left to drive back to the house, Brand retrieved his car from the clinic lot. Instead of going home, he drove to the church. Tonight he needed to pray for what was yet to come. At least he'd told Tom his plans, and his father-in-law assured him they would keep Austin at their house overnight. There was no need in going home late and then having to call Betsy back over so he could make the early morning delivery of the ransom the kidnapper demanded. Austin would be well cared for by his grandparents. He hoped by this time tomorrow to have Alex back safe at home.

Before leaving the hospital, Brand called their pastor to tell him of his plans. He no more than pulled onto the street when his phone rang. Absently, he picked it up and answered.

"Is everything all right up there, son?" his father greeted him.

He groaned inwardly before answering his father's question. In all the excitement of the day, he hadn't called his parents to tell them of the birth of their granddaughters, to say nothing of the disappearance of their grandson.

"Oh God, Dad, no. Nothing is all right. It won't ever be all right again."

"We heard about the kidnapping on television. They weren't giving out any names, but the description of the child fit Alex perfectly. What happened? Is there anything we can do? We can be there in—"

"No Dad, there's nothing you can do. Please don't come. It will only add to the confusion."

He went on to relate the happenings of the day. Describing it to his father, the whole thing sounded like the plot of a really bad cop show on television.

"They thought I was involved," he concluded after glancing in his mirror and seeing the unmarked car following him from the hospital to the church.

After promising to keep his parents apprised of what was happening, Brand closed the phone and pulled into the parking lot of the church. As he did, he saw the pastor's car already there. Even though darkness was falling, the dusk to dawn light illuminated the entire parking area.

True to form, the officers assigned to follow his every move pulled in behind him. Without acknowledging them, he got out of his car and hurried into the sanctuary.

"Are you all right?" Pastor Wolf spoke, as soon as Brand entered the building.

"You're the second person to ask me that in the last few minutes," he replied. "I'm afraid nothing will ever be all right. I thank you for opening the church for me. I really needed to come here and pray. I couldn't stand going home without Jenny and Alex there."

"What about Austin?"

"Tom and Betsy have taken him over to their house for the night. Since they have police protection at the hospital for Jenny and are following my every move, I'm certain they're at the house as well. Damn it, Pastor, why is something like this happening to Alex? What did he ever do wrong? What if he's no longer alive?"

The last question came as a surprise when it passed his lips. He hadn't wanted to think of anything happening to Alex and yet he now echoed the question Jenny asked him earlier.

"You must know this isn't God's will. We humans have been given free will, and sometimes God can only watch as we make our mistakes. Unfortunately, our free will often hurts innocents like Alex. I've been praying for his safety ever since I heard of the abduction. Would you like to join me in prayer?"

Brand nodded. He hardly realized they walked up to the altar as they talked. Without further prompting, he dropped to his knees and bowed his head in prayer. To his horror, the words wouldn't come.

As though Pastor Wolf read his mind, he began to pray aloud. The rambling prayer incorporated Alex, Jenny and the girls, Austin, Tom and Betsy, and Ben and Charlie. The prayer continued to ask for blessings on Brand and pleaded for the kidnapper to be compassionate toward Alex and to turn himself in before any harm came to Alex. It finally ended with the familiar A-Men, but Brand made no move to rise from his knees.

"I understand you need some time alone," Pastor Wolf said. "If you need me, I'll be in my office."

Brand lifted his head. "Thank you, Pastor. I do need to be alone."

Once the pastor left the sanctuary, Brand moved from his knees to one of the pews. Sitting alone, he allowed his mind to run wild. Behind his closed eyes, he saw Alex, alone with a madman, frightened beyond belief. The fear of something happening prompted Charlie's release from prison, not a week later. No one thought any child on the reservation could completely disappear while on a nature hike. Whoever this monster was, he held Alex away from the security of his family, but why? The only answer to come to mind was money and made Brand cringe in fear for the safety of his son. Jenny was right, once the man got what he wanted, he would have no further use for Alex. His son would become a disposable asset.

Someone touched his shoulder and the ramblings of his mind ceased. Opening his eyes, he saw an officer standing behind him.

"I hate to intrude on your prayers, Doctor, but it's time for you to get to the community center."

Brand recognized the young man. He must have relieved the last shift of officers guarding him sometime through the night. A glance at his watch told him it was four-thirty in the morning. He'd been at the church for over seven hours. How the entire night had passed without him even knowing it was beyond him.

Exhaustion and hunger plagued his body, but rest and food were the least of his worries. Until Alex was safely home, such luxuries meant nothing to him.

In the parking lot, a police cruiser sat next to Brand's car. He expected to see the young officer's partner, but seeing Charlie sitting in the back seat of the car came as a surprise.

"What are you doing here," he asked, when Charlie got out of the car.

"They got me out of prison to be your tracker. If this bastard gets away from the cops when you hand over the money, I'll be ready to track him to where he's holding Alex."

Brand nodded, remembering his father-in-law saying Charlie was one of the best trackers he'd ever trained. Brand prayed incarceration hadn't dulled Charlie's skills over the past four years.

"Tom told me you were one of the best he ever trained. Do you think you can still do it, if need be?"

"I'm Chippewa. It's something you don't forget. I'm not saying I'm a throw back to my ancestors, but I am good at tracking. It's like riding a bike. Once you know how to do it, it comes back when you need it, and God knows I need it this morning."

Without further conversation, Brand took the satchel of money from the officer who held it out to him and got into his car for the drive to the community center.

The sun hadn't quite crested the eastern horizon when Brand got out of his car in the parking lot. The closer he got to the building, the more his eyes adjusted to the early morning light. A man stepped from the shadows, but the nylon stocking he'd pulled over his head obscured his features.

"Did you bring the money, 'White Eyes'?" the man demanded, his voice muffled by the makeshift mask he wore.

"Yes. Where's my son?"

"Your son? How can you call a Chippewa boy your son?"

"Because I adopted him, and I love him. If you've hurt him, so help me…" He lunged toward the man.

The sound of an explosion accompanied the instant pain of the bullet slamming into his chest. He hadn't seen the gun the man carried. His last conscious thought was of Alex, Jenny, Austin, and the twins. For a brief moment, he prayed his family would be kept safe.

Chapter Nineteen

Charlie sat in the back of the cruiser and watched Brand walk across the parking lot to the shadowed area surrounding the community center.

The night of the sledding party replayed itself in Charlie's mind. After talking to Jenny, he knew she would be coming to the hill behind the community center, and he planned to confront her there. He'd heard she was seeing a white man, and the thought of her with anyone other than himself drove him out of his mind with jealousy. It wasn't like he actually wanted to marry her, but he didn't want anyone else to be with her either.

The memory of the bite of the whiskey he'd consumed prior to coming reminded him he couldn't handle his liquor. When he drank, he always ended up in more trouble than he needed. The rage at seeing her with a white man had led to violence and landed him in prison for the past four years.

Rather than dwell on the past, he focused on the past twenty-four hours. Yesterday morning, he'd awakened to the memory of Jenny not taking his call the night before. He decided to try to call her again, and for the first time he heard his son's voice. The terror at having his father call him collect was evident in his son's one word answer to the question of whether he would accept the charges. Alex's 'No!' echoed over and over again in Charlie's mind.

How could it have been less than six hours later when the guards told him someone kidnapped Alex and questioned his part in it? Thank goodness, the authorities believed him and allowed him to return home to aid in the search for the man who took Alex and was holding him hostage.

"Do you see someone near the building?" the young officer Charlie knew as Billy Tall Elk said.

Charlie again concentrated on the building Brand slowly approached. He watched as a man emerged from the shadows and took the satchel from Brand. To Charlie's shock, Brand reached out to grab the shirt of the man. The events following Brand's actions moved in slow motion. He saw the flash from the barrel of the gun before he actually heard the explosion. When Brand slumped to the ground, Charlie was out of the car like a shot, but the man who pulled the trigger disappeared back into the shadows and away from their view.

The first to get to Brand's side, Charlie could see the blood staining the front of Brand's white shirt. He knew it was, at one time, perfectly pressed, but now it was wrinkled and had a huge hole from where the bullet had torn through the material to reach its final resting place in Brand's chest. He put his fingers to Brand's neck and was relieved to feel a weak pulse.

"Get an ambulance out here," Charlie yelled. "I'm going after the bastard who has Alex."

Before anyone could stop him, he left Brand's side and rounded the corner of the building. It was clear the man behind this didn't know how to move through the forest without leaving a trail. It was as though a herd of blind buffalo had trampled through the underbrush looking for food.

Adrenaline pumped through Charlie forcing the fatigue of the past twenty-four hours from him. The now fully risen sun illuminated the sparsely forested area making the trail easier to follow.

The trees thinned even more, opening to a clearing in the forest. Charlie stopped short of the tree line and surveyed the area. In the center of the grassy area stood a teepee. The kidnapper apparently came prepared to the point of having the materials needed to build his own hideout, one he could dismantle with little effort and disappear easily.

He reached to his shoulder and touched the button on the police radio they'd issued him at the station. "I've found where he's holding Alex."

Charlie prayed the information he imparted would prove to be correct. After giving the officers behind him the information of where the clearing was located, he continued to watch.

As though on cue, he saw the door flap of the lodge open. It came as no surprise to see Preston come out of the dwelling, pulling a young boy along as he did. Charlie glanced around and saw an older pickup truck waiting for Preston to make his getaway.

Knowing once Preston got into the truck, there would be no way to keep up with him on foot. He reached into his boot and retrieved the hunting knife he'd secured there last evening. As an ex-con, there was no way the cops were going to give him a gun, but they didn't know about the knife. He at least had a way to defend himself.

"Let the boy go, Preston," Charlie said as he stepped into the clearing.

"Charlie, I didn't think you'd be out until next week. I got enough money for the two of us to start over again in Mexico. I even got the kid for you. We don't have to worry about White Eyes anymore. I took care of your problem with him for you."

"This isn't what I want, Preston. I'm not the kind of father Alex needs. Let him go. Now."

"I did this for you, man. Your old man even came up with the money. Do you know how well we can live in Mexico on two hundred thousand dollars?"

Charlie stepped closer to Preston, as though he planned to go along with this madman's plan. "Let me make certain this boy is my son," he said, holding out his left hand. His right hand gripped the handle of the hunting knife he held behind his back.

"Quit the bullshit, Charlie. This is your kid. If it wasn't, your old man wouldn't have come up with the money." Preston's grip on Alex's arm tightened.

Charlie moved close enough to see the fear in his son's eyes. Not only did Alex fear his captor, but his rescuer as well. He didn't blame the boy who probably considered Charlie little more than the boogieman who harmed his mother four years earlier and spent time in the state prison in Waupun.

Before Charlie was close enough to grab Alex's arm, Preston raised his gun. "Maybe the kid and I don't need you sharing all this money with us."

At the threat, Charlie brought up his right arm, knife in hand, and slashed at Preston's arm. "Run Alex," he shouted.

Preston dropped the gun and his grip on Alex eased. Even though the boy's hands were still tied, he pulled away and sprinted into the trees.

The gun fell to the ground, but Preston wasn't ready to give up so easily. He lunged at Charlie and knocked the knife from his hand.

Blood gushed from the wound on Preston's arm, but it didn't stop him from pounding Charlie's face with his right hand. Charlie hoped back up from the officers he had called on the radio came quickly. Exhaustion was taking its toll on Charlie. That coupled with Preston's muscular body put him at a disadvantage in this fight.

* * * *

The sound of sirens woke Jenny from a restless sleep. A glance at the clock on the wall opposite her bed told her it was less than an hour later than the appointed time for Brand to deliver the ransom to Alex's kidnapper. Had something gone wrong? If the kidnapper were badly injured or worse yet even dead, would they ever find Alex?

The PA system came alive with calls for nurses as well as a surgeon to come to the emergency room. Someone knocked on her door before pushing it open. She expected to see the morning nurse coming in to take her vitals. Instead, the officer who spent the night outside her door entered.

"There's been a shooting, Mrs. Masterson," he said.

Jenny's heart dropped to the pit of her stomach. "Alex?" She could hardly able say her son's name.

"No, Mrs. Masterson, we haven't found the boy yet. They just brought your husband into the emergency room. It would be best if you go down and see him before they take him up to surgery."

Jenny jumped out of bed not concerned about the officer getting a bird's eye view through the open back of her hospital gown. She hardly noticed when he turned his back allowing her privacy as she found the hospital issued robe and put on her slippers. A glance in the mirror told her she should have taken time to run a comb through her hair, but appearance was the least of her worries.

Last night she had mentally accused Brand of organizing Alex's disappearance. With the pain of her labor, she'd even said that to him. She knew it hurt him as much as the thought of his betrayal hurt her.

Although she wanted to protest, a nurse came with a wheelchair to take her down to the emergency room on the lower level of the hospital. She knew it was policy, but didn't always agree with it.

Once they wheeled her into the cubical in the emergency room where teams of doctors and nurses worked on Brand, tears burned her eyes. As soon as she saw him, Jenny was grateful to be sitting in the wheelchair. Had she been standing, she knew her knees would have buckled and she would have slumped to the floor.

Brand's white shirt lay in a bloody pile on the floor along with his suit. A sheet covered his lower body and a pressure bandage covered the right side of his chest where dried blood clung to the hair and skin of his chest. She breathed a sigh of relief when she realized the bandage wasn't on the left, meaning his heart hadn't been hit. If that were the case, people wouldn't be working so hard to save his life.

"Has he been conscious," she asked, the nurse in her taking control, pushing the emotional wife to the background.

"No," Hawk replied, "but I thought you should see him before we take him up to surgery,"

"How ... how bad is it?" she managed to say.

"I won't lie to you, Jenny. It's bad. The bullet didn't hit the heart, but I'm fairly sure it nicked his right lung. I won't know much more until I get in and see what we're looking at. Normally I wouldn't have allowed the wife to come in here, but you and I go back a long way. I thought you should see him before he goes up, just in case..."

Hawk didn't have to finish what he was saying. By looking at Brand, she knew it was possible he wouldn't survive the surgery. What if he died and didn't know how sorry she was for suspecting him last night? How could she live with the guilt, to say nothing of raising their kids alone?

She allowed the nurse to wheel her back to her room. When she got there her parents, as well as Brand's parents and Pastor Wolf waited for her.

"Who's watching Austin?" she demanded as soon as the nurse helped her get back into bed.

"He's in his glory," her mother replied. "Matt and Karen got here yesterday afternoon. They left right after I called to tell them you were having the twins and Alex was missing. Then last night, Doug and Leslie arrived. As for Brand's family, they all arrived early this morning. Did you get to see him?"

"Oh Mom, it's not good. Brand wasn't conscious. He was delivering the ransom money for Alex when the kidnapper shot him. They only let me see him because ... because they don't know if he's going to make it." She hated saying that in front of her mother-in-law, but it had to be said. She couldn't leave it hanging there for everyone to form their own conclusions. It was always better to be truthful with families, even when it was her family and their feelings were way too close to the surface.

Chapter Twenty

Charlie lay back against the gurney as the ambulance rushed toward the hospital. Behind him, another ambulance carried Preston and ahead of him. Alex rode in a police car.

Before reinforcements showed up, he'd taken one hell of a beating at Preston's hands. He was pretty sure his nose and several ribs were broken from the assault. The only thing to stop the beating from the much larger man was the arrival of the officers he'd called. Through it all, he'd heard Alex's fear filled sobs. He prayed the boy wouldn't be hurt either physically or mentally.

The ambulance stopped, and orderlies rushed to pull the gurney with Charlie on it from the back. They hurried him into the emergency room.

"I'm fine," he protested. "I want to know how Alex and Dr. Masterson are."

"Lay still, Charlie," the paramedic who treated him at the scene ordered. "We need to get you into x-ray so we can check on your ribs as well as your face. Broken bones are nothing to dismiss too lightly."

"What about Alex?"

"He's with the officers. From what we could tell when we checked him over, there were no injuries other than rope burns on his wrists."

Even something as innocent as rope burns on the boy's wrists was more than Charlie wanted for his son. He should have remained innocent of the ways of the world. Instead, a madman held him captive, and Charlie blamed himself. If he hadn't been so angry when he first went to prison. If only he hadn't he vented that anger to his cellmate, none of this would have happened. He'd had no idea Preston was capable of something this heinous until after he'd been moved from Charlie's cell.

It was only a matter of moments before an orderly wheeled him into an examination room. With the help of a nurse, they transferred him from the gurney to the bed and propped the head portion of the bed so he could breathe easier. He wished he could ask to have the cervical collar removed, but it would be an exercise in futility. He'd already asked the paramedics to take it off in the ambulance and they refused. They'd said something about him possibly having a head injury and not wanting to make anything worse. At least that's what he thought they said. He was pretty fuzzy on the details about anything since the beating from Preston.

After what seemed like an eternity, someone knocked at the door. He didn't bother to answer the knock because whoever was on the other outside would enter anyway.

"I have someone here who wants to see you,"

Charlie looked toward the door at the sound of his father's voice. With him was Alex. He'd seen the boy only briefly in the clearing. He took a moment to study him more closely. Seeing him now, was like looking into a twenty-year-old mirror. He wondered how Jenny had stood the daily reminder of how he'd treated her when she told him she was carrying his child.

"Grandpa Ben says you're my father," Alex said.

Tears welled in Charlie's eyes. "I fathered you, but Dr. Masterson is your dad."

"I know. Dad and I talked about it the other night after you called the house. How did you find me? I didn't think anyone could find us as far out in the woods as he took me."

"I had a good man teach me how to track when I was your age."

Alex looked up at Charlie's dad with admiration in his eyes.

"It wasn't me," Ben confessed. "It was your Grandpa Red Hawk. He was the scoutmaster for Charlie's Boy Scout troop. You have him to thank for Charlie's expertise."

The admiration in Alex's eyes warmed Charlie's heart. It had been a long time since anyone had reason to admire him. The last time he could remember was in high school when he made the winning touchdown at the homecoming game.

"I think your mom is anxious to see you," Charlie said before he lost it completely. His emotions were in knots over the look in his son's eyes.

"Can you teach me to track?" Alex said, refusing to move.

"Only if it's all right with your parents. I don't have any rights to be with you and—"

"And you saved me from that man. I know I have a father, but I'd like you to be my friend."

Charlie wanted his son to leave him alone. He certainly didn't want Alex to see him cry.

"Charlie's right," Ben said. "All of this can wait. Your mom and grandparents are upstairs waiting for you. It's time you went to see them and to meet your new sisters.

Alex's eyes lit up. "Mom had the twins?"

"They were born yesterday. They're all doing well. I went to see them early this morning. There was nothing else I could do. I couldn't be out there looking for you. I knew Charlie would find you. I had to tell your mother you'd be all right."

The boy nodded and allowed Ben to lead him from the room. Then and only then did Charlie give in to the tears threatening to fall for the last half hour. His anger almost cost his son his life. Why hadn't he come to grips with what he did to Jenny before things went so far? He hurt her on the day he refused to step up to the plate and be a father to her son. At the time, he'd had a bright future. Bright until he messed everything up in college.

* * * *

With the grandparents down at the nursery oohing and ahhing over the babies, Jenny took a moment to rest. If things were different, Brand would be taking her home today. Instead, she felt as though her world had suddenly collapsed. The girls were too small to go home, Alex was missing, and Brand remained in surgery. Austin appeared to be the only normal person in their family.

For the second time since she woke this morning, the officer stationed outside her door came into the room. "It's over," he advised her.

Fear clutched at Jenny's heart. She didn't dare look at the officer. If he knew the worst had happened, she would be able to read it in his eyes.

"They just brought in your son, the kidnapper, and Charlie Little Horse. They're all down in the emergency department."

"My son, how is my son?" she pleaded, looking up to see the officer's smile.

"Other than some rope burns on his wrists, I'm told he suffered no injuries."

She breathed a sigh of relief. "How long before I can see him?"

"Ben Little Horse was waiting for them to arrive. I'm told he'll be bringing the boy up to see you as soon as the doctors give him a full exam."

Behind the officer, Jenny saw her parents along with Brand's enter the room. "Did you hear that? Alex is safe. He'll be coming up here as soon as they make certain he's all right."

"I heard," her father replied. "I also heard Ben Little Horse is bringing him up here. I'd rather go down and get Alex myself."

"Please, Dad, don't. Ben loves Alex as much as you do. Just because Charlie's his son doesn't make him the enemy. He's been very supportive of us. Let him have this time alone with Alex."

"I don't mind Ben having time alone with the boy. What I don't want is for him to take Alex to see Charlie."

"I think your grandson has every right to officially meet the man who saved his life," the officer said. "I know what the connection is, but the truth of the matter is, if it wasn't for Charlie Little Horse, we don't know what would have happened to the boy."

Jenny thought back to the conversation she'd had with her father last evening. He'd admitted Charlie was the best tracker he had ever trained. If Charlie did save Alex, the tracking ability her father taught him was the tool he'd used. It didn't matter to Jenny what part Charlie played in Alex's rescue. Her son was safe and life would soon return to normal.

"I have someone here who wants to see you," Ben said as he entered the room.

Jenny looked up to see Alex. His eyes belied his lack of sleep, and his hair looked the way it did every morning when he got out of bed and hadn't combed it.

"Mom, I'm so glad to be away from that bad man," Alex said as he rushed toward the bed to be enfolded in her arms.

"I am too."

"My new friend, Charlie, saved me. He said it was because Grandpa Red Hawk taught him to be a tracker. Can Charlie and Grandpa teach me how to track?"

"Your dad and I will have to talk about that."

"I know, that's what Charlie said when I asked him. When I asked him if he was my father, he got real sad. He said he fathered me but he wasn't my dad."

Fear about what Charlie might have told Alex turned to joy. If she could believe her son, Charlie hadn't come back to the reservation to make trouble for her and Brand.

"Can you take some more good news?" Hawk said from behind the group of people surrounding Jenny and Alex.

"Good news?" Jenny's voice was little more than a whisper.

"Brand is out of surgery. He was very lucky. Even though the bullet nicked his right lung, we were able to repair the damage and no other organs were hit. One of his ribs stopped the bullet and the surgery was a complete success. He'll be in the hospital about as long as your twins, but he's going to be all right. It looks like God and the Great Spirit were looking out for him today."

* * * *

Conscious thought returned to Brand. Around him, monitors beeped telling him doctors and nurses were monitoring his condition.

"You were very lucky, Dr. Masterson," a nurse he didn't recognize said.

"What happened?" he managed to ask.

Hawk came into his line of vision. "You were shot, Brand."

Memories of the events of yesterday filled his mind. The last thing he remembered was leaving the church to deliver the ransom the kidnapper had demanded for his son.

"Alex?"

"He wasn't hurt. While I was waiting for you to wake up from surgery, I went to Jenny's room. The two of them looked very happy. I'm told his only injuries, other than being hungry and tired, were the rope burns on his wrists. They're both concerned about you, but I assured them you're going to be back to your old ornery self in a couple of weeks."

Brand smiled at his friend's teasing. It meant once everything went back to normal they'd have only the memories of this event as a reminder of what transpired over the past couple of days.

* * * *

By the next morning, Brand felt stronger. Several people, including his parents, Jenny's parents, Jenny, Alex, Ben, and Charlie had visited.

"I hear Charlie Little Horse has been in to see you," Hawk said, after he made his morning examination. "Have the two of you buried the hatchet?"

The mental picture of one or the other of them burying a tomahawk in the other's skull brought a smile to Brand's lips. "There's nothing to bury. Charlie saved my son's life, and he and Jenny have made amends. He's made it clear he doesn't want to be anything more than a friend to Alex. I have no problem with him being back in the area."

"That's good. I knew Charlie when he played football for the local high school team. He was one hell of a good linebacker, just not good enough to make it in college. I think the realization came as the first of many blows to his ego.

Chapter Twenty-one

Brand admitted he was far from the best patient in the hospital. He found fault with the food and snapped at the nurses when they came in to make him get up to walk the halls.

"Are you ready to go home," Hawk asked after he finished his daily examination. "I told Jenny I planned to keep you until the twins were ready to go home, but I didn't think it was fair to send her home with three babies. Besides, I've received complaints from every nurse on the floor about you."

"The nurses are right. I haven't been the best patient in the world. Besides, I've been telling you I needed to go home for the past several days, Doc. I can't believe you insisted you keep me here this long. It's been over a week. We never keep patients that long."

Hawk laughed. "We only keep the special patients that long. I know you're more than ready to leave here, just remember, you aren't as strong as you think you are. Being at home is entirely different from being in the hospital."

The reminder brought a smile to Brand's lips. "You sound like me when I'm dismissing a patient. I know the pitfalls of going home and overdoing things. Do you know how much longer before the twins will be home?"

"They'll be dismissed by the end of the week. They're both gaining weight, and their lungs have developed. I arranged for you to be taken up to see them before Jenny takes you home. I know you've been anxious to get up to the nursery, but until now, I didn't think you were strong enough. I also didn't want to risk any infections passing between you and the girls."

"You're right, of course, but I'm anxious to see them. I didn't even get to hold them after they were born. They whisked me down to the police station the minute they were both born and in their incubators. I've got more than a week of bonding to make up."

Hawk smiled. "I think you'll get plenty of diaper duty, since I'm not releasing you to go back to work for at least another month. From what I hear between your mother and Betsy, Jenny will have lots of help with you and the girls."

"I know. Jenny told me my folks are planning to come up as soon as the girls are released from the hospital, and of course Betsy comes over every day making certain Jenny rests and Austin is cared for. We're lucky to have such good parents."

"There's one more thing I want to talk to you about."

"I think I know what that is. Charlie Little Horse has been to visit me every day I've been here. He's here to stay, and Jenny and I have to deal with it."

"I talked to him too. He assured me he doesn't want to take your place with Alex, but he did rescue him. I think they've formed a special bond."

"I do too. As for Alex, he's been a bit of a celebrity at school as well. The kids used to tease him about being a bastard, but after the kidnapping, his status has come up a couple of notches. Before all of this started, he told us about the teasing. I'd planned to talk to his teachers when all hell broke loose. I certainly didn't want something like this to happen to him, but I'm glad to hear he's more accepted now than he was before."

They talked for several more minutes before Hawk told Brand he needed to visit the patients who were really sick. Within less than a half an hour, he was seated in a wheelchair and heading toward the nursery.

He found Jenny waiting for him outside the glass separating them from their babies.

"It's good to see you out and about," she said as she bent to give him a hug and a kiss. "Hawk told me you're ready to go home today. I called your folks, and they're on their way here as we speak."

"Are you sure you're up to dealing with my parents?"

"It won't be so bad. They're staying with Mom and Dad, like they did when they came up here last week. Everyone else has gone home and life is mainly back to normal. Do you want to go in and hold the twins?"

"You know I do. They took me out of here so fast on the day the girls were born, I didn't even get a chance to let either of them grab on to my finger, to say nothing of holding them."

Jenny took the handles of Brand's wheelchair and pushed him toward the door to the nursery held open by one of the nurses.

"It's good you can finally get to see the girls, Dr. Masterson," the nurse said, once the door closed behind him.

"It's good to be here." He allowed Jenny to help him put on a sterile gown and wheel him over to wash his hands before handling the twins.

Anne was the first placed in his arms. Her coppery complexion combined with her black hair left no doubt of her Chippewa heritage. To his surprise, her bright blue eyes attested to his part in her conception. It came as a surprise they hadn't turned brown, but he knew they would eventually. Brown was the dominant gene after all.

Once he was comfortable with her cradled in his right arm, the nurse handed him Anne's carbon copy, Amy. Like her sister, her eyes were still blue. Their color added to the exotic beauties the girls would grow up to be. He knew it was an impossible dream, but he wished they would remain light like his.

"They're beautiful," he whispered. "Hawk says they can come home soon. It can't be soon enough for me."

"Maybe not for you, but I'm the one who has to get up at two in the morning for their feedings. I know what you mean, though. I want them home as badly as you do. I don't think we'll have to worry too much about taking care of them. My mother is itching to get her hands on the girls, and I know your mother feels the same."

* * * *

By two, Jenny wondered if bringing Brand home today had been such a good idea. She knew coming home would be tiring, but she hadn't expected to see her strong husband collapse, completely exhausted, in the recliner as soon as they returned home.

While he'd been in the hospital, she hadn't noticed the weight loss. Seeing Brand dressed in jeans and a tee shirt, Jenny realized just what a toll the shooting had taken on his body. Beneath the thin material of the shirt, she could see the outline of the heavy bandage covering the incision in his chest that closed the surgical opening they'd made to remove the bullet threatening his life.

Jenny knew she should be preparing something for their supper, but she didn't have the strength. She closed her eyes, giving thanks for her nurse training. It would enable her to keep a close watch on the incision as it healed.

It would be another few days before Hawk or one of the other doctors would be removing the staples. Until then, she had to be on her guard against any kind of infection.

She didn't realize how tired she was until she slipped into the sweet bliss of sleep. With Brand home, she relaxed for the first time since the nightmare of Alex's kidnapping.

* * * *

The sound of the screen door opening brought Brand to full attention. He glanced at Jenny sleeping peacefully on the couch. Looking toward the door, he saw Alex enter the living room. Rather than disturb Jenny, Brand put his finger to his lips.

In acknowledgement, Alex nodded and hurried to Brand's side. Careful to stand on Brand's left to avoid the area of his injury, Alex put his arms around his father's neck.

"I'm so glad you're home, Dad," he whispered in Brand's ear.

The words brought a smile to his lips. Earlier he'd seen Austin before Betsy took him across the driveway to her place. His parents came in right after Austin left. Now with Alex home, Brand knew his world was complete.

A week ago, Charlie Little Horse threatened this home, this place of peace and perfection. Charlie's early release from prison came because of Alex's kidnapping, and he rescued Alex when the kidnapper's bullet threatened to take Brand's life.

So much changed in the span of only a few hours. From now on Brand would be Alex's father of choice and Charlie his father of chance.

Together, they would make certain the future for Alex would be as bright as it would be for the rest of Brand and Jenny's children.

About the Author

Mild Mannered wife, mother, and grandmother by day, Sherry Derr-Wille spends her nights writing and writing and writing. Having been inspired by an English assignment in her sophomore year of high school, she had never quite finished the assignment. New stories pop into her head every day with never enough time to write them all.

A Wisconsin native, she grew up a country girl, but enjoys her 'city' home. She and her husband of 50 years, Bob, live in a mid-sized town close to the Illinois border, where they are both enjoying their retirement. Deeming Bob 'A Saint' for putting up with her she has never regretted marrying her high school sweetheart just two days after graduation in 1964.

www.derr-wille.com

Read more by this author at
www.melange-books.com

Family Secrets
Hattie's Preacher, The Outlaw Series, Book 1
Outlaw's Son, The Outlaw Series, Book 2
Outlaw's Daughter, The Outlaw Series, Book 3
Outlaw's Secrets, The Outlaw Series, Book 4

www.ingramcontent.com/pod-product-compliance
Lightning Source LLC
Chambersburg PA
CBHW032012240626
47153CB00003B/1229